Durand Lassois received Joan with the fussy kindness that distinguished him, and she lost no time in asking him for help.

'I need a safe conduct from the Governor so that I can leave the province.'

'Leave the province? Child, what madcap scheme have you in your head?'

'A plan, cousin, not a wild scheme. You must have heard the tradition about the virgin who will come out of Lorraine to save France.'

'Everybody has heard that tale,' Durand said, puzzled.

Joan took a deep breath, walked over to the small window opening into the narrow street. 'Cousin, I am that virgin,' she said simply.

MAUREEN PETERS

Joan of the Lilies

Collins

FONTANA BOOKS

First published by Robert Hale & Co. 1969
First issued in Fontana Books 1972

© Maureen Peters 1969

Printed in Great Britain
Collins Clear-Type Press
London and Glasgow

CHAPTER ONE

DOMREMY, JANUARY 1412

THEY had tied his hands together, but the chafing of the rope around his wrists was less troublesome than the pain in his buttocks as they were rubbed back and forth on the badly-fitting saddle with every movement of the horse.

Giles, who had a low opinion of horses, cursed, and attempted to shift his position. The man who held the leading rein glanced over his shoulder.

'Soon we will stop and water the animals,' he called.

Not a word about my discomfort, Giles thought indignantly. We've been riding for hours without a break but these damned Frenchmen have no pity on my tortured limbs. Then his natural sense of fair play asserted itself. He was, after all, a prisoner and they had treated him with unusual leniency. Even their putting him on a horse had not savoured of malice as they could not be expected to know that Giles preferred his own two feet to the more sophisticated forms of transport. One or two of them even spoke English, after a fashion. Giles, who had never troubled to learn any foreign language, took this as a natural compliment to the superiority of his own tongue.

He wished they had not taken his bow away. He had carried the weapon for four years ever since his sixteenth birthday and he felt naked without the familiar weight of it across his back. He had carved the wood himself, lovingly polishing and shaping through a hundred evenings, while his clumsy boy's hands took unto themselves some of the grace and beauty of the materials on which he worked.

When the bow was finished he had risen and stood before his mother and she had seen, with pain in her heart, how the child who once clung to her skirts needed now to stoop lest his head catch on the wooden beams of the roof. But she had said nothing because she wished him to return, and she had already learned that it was essential to hold what is precious with open hands. This time it was harder, because Giles was the last of her five sons and the most impatient. She could not blame them for wishing to leave the sleepy hamlet where a few families scraped a living from poor pasture, but if only one of them had been content to stay!

Silently she raised her hand to bless him, and he had gone through the open door and along the track with his loping, youthful gait, and she sat still until his footsteps had died away before she went through to the shed where the cow waited to be milked.

Giles had been home twice in the next four years and he had brought presents and coins which he had kept back for her from his share of the plunder with which bowmen supplemented their meagre pay. But he was no longer a lad. He was an archer in the service of Sir Atholl Beaumont and no female could lay claim to him. She had hoped he might settle down as two of his older brothers had done and take a wife, but he showed little interest in any of the village girls although they eyed him invitingly, and, every time he left, the winter evenings seemed longer and colder to her.

For no apparent reason Giles thought suddenly of the warm, smoky room where a skinned coney or a young chicken usually swung over the fire, and his mother rose from time to time to baste the animal with lard, while on the shelf the bowls and spoons waited.

'My stomach cleaves to my backbone!' he said, aloud, but nobody answered him.

For the first time he wondered why they had kept him alive. It was probably in the hope of ransom but surely these French fools had the sense to know that only officers could raise enough money for their release. Mercenaries might rot for years in prison, so it was more usual to kill them at once and save the expense of feeding them.

Giles hoped they didn't intend to get information out of him for he had none to give. Sir Atholl, having raided several chateaux in Champagne had decided to make for the coast where his ship waited. A few of the younger men had voted to march further up country to the borders of Lorraine and join their companions later. Atholl, who kept the loyalty of his men by the simple expedient of allowing them to do pretty much as they pleased when the main objective of the raid was accomplished, agreed to delay his sailing for a week.

If we had not had the ill-luck to run into a scouting party, Giles thought savagely, and if it had not decided to rain so that my feet slithered and slipped! If! If!

Three of them had got away; two lay mute and cold, and Giles might be free at this instant had he not stopped to pick up his quiver and been surrounded, and tied up, and dumped on to this evil-jointed beast.

'We go to Vaucouleurs!' shouted the man who led the horse. 'There is to be an exchange of prisoners at Vaucouleurs.'

So he was to be handed back in return for a scurvy Frenchman! Such bargains were sometimes struck between various raiding parties. His stomach muscles loosened with relief and he was even more aware of his hunger.

'Will there be anything to eat at this Vau—what you said?'

'Vaucouleurs! Do you English think of nothing but your appetites?'

'Only of killing Frenchmen!' he retorted, and braced himself for a blow, but his captors merely laughed, translating the remark among themselves.

The rain had eased off a little, but the ground was still treacherous with pools of cracked ice in the ruts of the road. The country was bleak and barren, frozen in winter, and the few people they met turned hastily aside.

They rode through a cobbled square with a dozen or so peasants grouped about a stake. Giles craned his neck and saw an old woman sagging there in chains. She seemed unconscious or dead but they were piling faggots about her and chattering. A priest stood near, and as the horsemen slowed their pace he hurried up to the leader of them and spoke rapidly, stamping his feet to rebuke the cold.

'The place is bewitched by the old woman,' the Frenchman told Giles. 'The good father says there is no water in the wells nor milk in the cows. When she is burnt, the spell will be removed, but he tells me there will be water for the horses at Domremy if we go a very little out of our way.'

They had kindled the faggots now, but the damp wood smouldered and some of the peasants moved away, coughing as white smoke swirled up, feathering the unconscious woman. Hastily prisoner and captors crossed themselves and made the sign against the evil eye, and then they were spurring their horses across open country again and the column of smoke hung behind them in the still air.

'You have many witches in England?' The Frenchman was eager to talk, as if to dispel the uneasiness that had fallen over the little group.

'Not many.'

'In France there are many—what is the word?—covens. They bring evil. It is better that they burn.'

Giles despised himself for hoping the old woman had been already dead, and nodded agreement.

Their paler shadows were long on the grass when they splashed across a shallow dyke and rode up the narrow twisting street ahead. It was a poor place, Giles decided, staring at the wooden huts and tiny stone cottages. There were a few rushlights already burning in the doorways of the larger houses but most of the windows were shuttered. Somewhere a child cried and was swiftly hushed.

'They think we may be Burgundians,' said the leader, amused, and raising his voice he shouted. Evidently his words were reassuring, because here and there bolts were drawn and a few people ventured cautiously into the street.

One of them, a blacksmith to judge by his physique, caught hold of the bridle and talked for several minutes in a low, earnest tone.

'They are not happy when strangers ride in, so they hide away like mice,' the French captain said scornfully. 'You will wait here until we return.'

One of the troop gave Giles a shove that sent him tumbling into the dusty road. Then the captain dismounted and went into one of the larger houses, while the rest of his company straggled up to the water-trough where the animals were soon slaking their thirst. Some of the villagers were coming out with bowls and leather cups to offer to the soldiers and the air was shrill with voices.

Giles picked himself up and leaned against a rail. His mind considered and rejected the possibility of flight; then he stretched his body feeling every muscle creak in protest. Nobody was staring at him openly but he sensed covert glances and an underlying air of hostility. He amused himself by imagining his mother's caustic comments if she could have seen the grimy doorsteps and the piles of dung in the gutter. These peasants took little pride in their homes, but then the entire village had a dilapidated, hopeless aspect.

A woman had moved out of the shadow of one of the cottages, and his attention was flicked when she came nearer and held out a bowl to him. There was soup in the vessel and he drank it greedily, surprised to find it hot and pleasantly flavoured. As he handed back the empty bowl, her gaze travelled slowly over his bound wrists where the flesh had rubbed raw.

She was not a particularly young woman, nor particularly attractive, being in the last stages of pregnancy, with a sallow skin and thin features. Then she raised her head and he was forced to admit to himself that her eyes were really rather beautiful. At first he had thought that they were dark, but as she came closer to take the bowl, he saw they were blue; so intense a blue that their very whites

9

were tinged with the shade. Their expression was even more remarkable, being at once innocent as childhood and wise as time, so he had the uncanny impression that the woman looked through him to the depths of his being and then beyond to a world he couldn't see.

Then somebody called, 'Zabillet! Zabillet!' and she moved away, pulling her scarf over her head and stepping ponderously among the dungheaps.

The captain was coming back, having evidently established his authority, for he was now doing all the talking while the powerfully built man listened, nodding respectfully.

Giles was hoisted reluctantly to his unwilling mount, and the rest of them were cramming the remains of bread and cheese into their mouths and climbing to their saddles with the unnecessary dash and vigour shown by all young men when there are girls to watch them.

'It will be very late when we reach Vaucouleurs,' the captain said to Giles, 'but they have no rooms to spare at this place, nor liking for visitors. And they hate the English almost as much as they hate Burgundians.'

'Goddam it! don't compare me to a Burgundian!' Giles exclaimed, crossly.

'I am glad you see it as an insult. There is hope for you yet, my friend.'

The captain looped the reins of the two horses through his fingers and raised his hand. A few ill-clad children ran squealing out of the path of the hoofs as the troop re-formed and wheeled south again.

There was no sign of the pregnant woman with the intent blue gaze, and the lowering sky threatened more sleet.

'A miserable hole!' Giles muttered, and felt disappointment mingle with irritation.

'As you say, Englishman. A miserable hole, fit only for serfs and peasants with no guts.' The captain spat accurately and contemptuously in the centre of the street. 'At

Vaucouleurs, you will find better accommodation. There is nothing worth seeing at Domremy.'

They ducked their heads against the gathering wind and rode into the twilight.

DOMREMY, NOVEMBER, 1415

Jean Morel shifted his weight from one foot to another and strained his eyes through the gathering dusk. From his position on the high wooden tower, he had a bird's eye view of the surrounding countryside, but he was uncomfortably aware that he provided an excellent target.

He pushed the thought away and gripped the edge of the rickety structure wishing that Thevenin would hurry. But Thevenin was not due to take his turn as outlook for another two hours; meanwhile Jean must remain where he was, perched uncomfortably above the fields and streams where, in the changing light, every bush took on the semblance of a crouching man.

There were rumours circulating. There were always rumours, but lately they had become more insistent and disturbing. The English King and the Dukes of Burgundy planned to join forces, went the murmur, so that they could invade France and divide the land between them. Nobody seriously expected Domremy to be invaded, but the older men in the village thought some token show of preparation ought to be put up. So the citizens, armed with billhook and scythe, took their turn as watchdogs. It had been exciting at first, with the hourly expectation of an enemy host marching against the skyline, but month followed month, and only when twilight distorted familiar shapes could the old anticipatory fear be recaptured.

Somebody was riding towards the tower. Jean tightened his throat muscles and prepared to give the high wailing cry that would warn the neighbourhood. Then he paused, remembering uncomfortably how the previous month he had seen just such a rider and had cried his warning, only to recognize the man as a cousin hurrying to fetch the priest for his dying grandmother. By the time they had reached Domremy, the sheep and cattle were being driven into the churchyard, three of the women were in hysterics having lost their children, and one over-enthusiastic warrior had already stabbed another in the leg.

As Jean hesitated, the rider pulled up his horse beneath the tower.

'How far to Vaucouleurs?'

'Too far to reach there before night,' Jean answered, thankful to recognize the French tongue.

The man swore, wiping his hand across the heaving flank of his mount.

'Domremy is near. I come from Domremy,' Jean said, anxious to be helpful.

The man still looked flustered and annoyed.

'I have papers to deliver to the Governor of Vaucouleurs,' he shouted up. 'Will there be a fresh horse at Domremy?'

'Not as fast as the one you sit.'

'No matter, so long as he be fresh, for this one has almost burst his heart with galloping.'

The rider dug his spurs into the exhausted animal, and Jean almost fell over the parapet in his curiosity.

'Do you bring bad news that you ride so speedily?' Jean enquired.

'A defeat! The English have won an important battle.'

The words were flung over his shoulder. Jean's eyes bulged with terror. Manning the watchtower had once seemed an amusing game. Now, in a landscape drained of colour, the game was sinister and fearsome.

When the messenger reached Domremy, he had a large audience eager to pay him the compliment of listening, with silent attention, to every word he uttered. The villagers relied for news upon proclamations and the gossip of pedlars and troubadours, and were eager to discover what brought a messenger on such urgent business to the

Governor of Vaucouleurs.

While a fresh horse was being saddled, he ate bread and salt mutton.

'The English King Henry won a great victory two weeks ago,' he told them between mouthfuls. 'Eleven thousand Frenchmen were killed. I said "battle" but it was more a massacre. The goddams fought like the sons of devils, ignoring all the rules of chivalry.'

'Where was this battle?' half a dozen voices questioned.

'At Agincourt.'

'I never heard of the place,' one greybeard said as if he doubted the existence of anything outside his personal experience.

'Everybody will remember the name now,' the messenger answered grimly, 'for the finest warriors of our land lie at Agincourt. And the goddams are pushing further inland, burning and looting as they come. I have sealed orders for the Governor.' He tapped the leather case he carried, waiting for the appropriate murmurs of awe, and went on with a due sense of his own importance. 'Of course, I am not permitted to reveal the exact nature of their contents, but I can tell you that extra troops are to be raised, and you would all do well to double the guard around your homes.'

'Do you think the goddams will come here?' squeaked a girl.

'Not very likely, but they are driving refugees before them. Men and women without homes or hope become dangerous animals.'

'What is a refugee?' piped a child's voice.

The messenger looked down into dark blue eyes questioning out of a round, rosy face. 'Refugees are people who lose their homes and have to run away when the goddams come,' he explained.

'And what are goddams?'

'The goddams are the English and are so called because they begin every sentence with a curse.'

'Why do they do that?'

'Because they have been badly brought up and allowed to interrupt their elders!' a woman said severely, catching the little girl by the shoulder. 'I must apologize for my daughter, sir, but she is over-forward for her age and we have spoiled her a little.'

The messenger smiled and waved his hand deprecatingly, saying that he had daughters of his own.

'How many?' asked the child.

'Three, but they are older than you are.'

'And better behaved, I'll warrant!' the woman added crossly. 'Now hold your tongue, Joan, and let your betters speak.'

'I have no more time for speech. I must ride on to Vaucouleurs.'

'Are you afraid that the goddams will catch you?' the child asked, round eyed.

'Will you be *quiet*, Joan! Sir, I have cousins in Vaucouleurs. Do you think they are in danger?'

'In a garrison town? Zabillet, don't be foolish.'

A thickset man had arrived on the fringe of the group and saluted the messenger.

'Jaques d'Arc, at your service, sir. Do you require escort to Vaucouleurs? It is unsafe to travel the district alone at night. We are so near the borders of Burgundy that there are frequent raids.'

'I will take my chance.'

The messenger stepped outside the cottage where he had been sitting and flung his leg over the waiting horse. He fumbled in his pouch and threw a florin carelessly into the air. Two plump hands enfolded it, but there followed an anguished squeal as Zabillet boxed her child's ears and Jacques d'Arc handed back the coin.

'We do not accept largess,' he said stiffly, 'and your horse is surety for the return of the one you have borrowed. Go in peace!'

'It was pretty and shiny,' Joan was roaring. 'It was pretty! I want it back!'

'You are not a beggar-child to grovel for charity in the road. Zabillet take the child indoors.'

'Come! You heard what your father said.'

Zabillet caught her wriggling daughter under her arm and carried her inside.

'You must not be so greedy,' she scolded, 'or you will become like the English and the Burgundians who are not content with what they have, but try to steal away what is not theirs.'

'The man gave it to me.'

'He threw it in the air so that you had to jump up for it like a dog who has no pride. You must not accept gifts given in that fashion. You are as good as anybody else, and you must not let people treat you as if you were not.'

'Yes, Mother,' Joan said, half-understanding.

'Then go up to bed now. The light has gone.'

'Goodnight, Mother.'

Joan, whose occasional storms of temper died as quickly as they arose, kissed her mother submissively and scurried up the ladder to the tiny room under the eaves where she slept.

There was space on the floor only for the mattress with its pile of woollen blankets. Joan crawled across to the round window with the bar across to prevent her falling out, and looked down into the street. People were still standing about in small groups, buzzing like bees and nodding their heads.

The man must have gone to Vaucouleurs. He had been an important man for he was on his way to see the governor, and Robert de Baudicourt was overlord of the whole district.

Joan didn't know exactly what an overlord was, but she was aware it was something grand and important. She knew he sent men round to collect money, and after the men had been, her father was always in a bad temper and grumbled about something called high taxation. On those occasions he frequently declared they would be ruined.

Joan had seen a ruined house once, burned down in a summer storm and she remembered the blackened stone and the big holes where the doors and roof had been. The house had looked like a face, with the skin burned off and the eyes empty. For a long time afterwards she used to dream that it grew legs, and got up and chased her all by itself, and as she fled, it shouted 'Taxation! Taxation!'

She closed her eyes tightly against the memory and listened instead to the church-bells, ringing out in the gloom. The bell-ringer often practised in the evenings and she liked to listen. The music was so high and joyful, sweeter even than the cowbells hung around the leaders of the herd.

When I was very little, Joan thought, I was sure angels rang the bells but it was only old Thiesselin whose nose has red lines all over it. Yet, perhaps when he tugs the long ropes, an angel comes and stands behind him and tells him what to do.

The thought amused her and she stuffed her fist in her mouth to stifle a giggle. She couldn't imagine anybody daring to tell Thiesselin what to do, for he had a fearsome temper. Even the bells obeyed him and gave out the sounds he wished them to produce, but if anybody else tried to work the ropes they jangled out of tune.

The smell of cooking and the low murmuring of voices drifted up the ladder. The street was empty now, but she could hear the clank of milk-pails and the sound of whistling as her big brother, Jacquemin, came from the byre.

Soon it will be Christmas, Joan thought—well, in a month or two—and we will eat goose and the yellow apples Mother has stored away. And I will have the new red dress she has been making, just as I do every year, and we will light a candle for the Child Jesus, and then we will all go down to the fairy-tree and hang holly over its branches, and the big boys and girls will hold hands and dance, and the little ones will clap in time, and Estellin will play his flute.

She jerked herself awake and hastily wriggled out of her dress. The blankets were scratchy and warm against her bare skin and the star outside her window was almost near enough to touch.

PARIS, APRIL, 1418

The youth in the velvet doublet studied his reflection gloomily in the mirror of polished steel. His suit was beautifully cut and stitched with gold and silver thread in a pattern of acorns, and his stockings were pure silk. Yet, not even the diamonds adorning his pointed shoes, nor the pearl-encrusted handle of his new dagger could disguise the fact that he was small, thin and so pale that, behind his back, the pages called him 'Cheeseface.'

'I am Charles de Valois, Dauphin of France,' he said, loudly, and his reedy voice echoed in the great chamber.

'Dauphin of what?'

His sister, Katharine had come in, and the teasing cadence of her voice caused him to flush miserably.

'Of France,' he said, stoutly, but his lip began to tremble.

'Of the bits of France that the English have not yet invaded,' she corrected scornfully.

'My armies will overcome them,' he said, grandly.

'Your armies, indeed. You can't afford to buy clothes for your own back, let alone equip soldiers. I'll wager the fine outfit you're wearing is one of Jean's cast-offs!'

'Not so! Jean never wore it!'

'But he paid for it?'

'I borrowed the money from him, but I fully intend to pay it back.'

'Hah!' Katharine curled her lip in the manner that the court gallants found irresistible, and made Charles wish it were permissible to hit one's sister.

Instead he began to complain.

'Is it my fault that I never have any money? You know

half the taxes we raise disappear in the pockets of the tax collectors. And our lady-mother keeps most of the money for her own use.'

'Or for her lovers,' Katharine sniggered but there was uneasiness in her mirth.

It was not healthy to joke about Queen Isabel, for she had the uncanny knack of hearing the merest whisper and of tracking every rumour to its source. Her children feared and disliked her and kept out of her way as much as possible.

Yet Charles, in his usual contrary fashion, attempted a feeble defence.

'She has not had an easy life, especially since father's last illness.'

'Last bout of madness, you mean! Why, that was the best stroke of luck she ever had for it gave her the chance to rule as she pleased, without any interference.'

'You always see things so clearly, Katharine,' Charles sighed. 'You look every fact in the face and you don't shrink away.'

'That's because I'm a woman and they are not as sentimental as men.'

It was true, he thought, looking at seventeen-year-old Katharine. Although she was only two years older than he was she had a steady gaze and a way of lifting her small chin as if she defied the world to do its worst. And he had never seen her cry. Charles cried a great deal, often in private but sometimes even in public where it was impossible to disguise one's sobs.

'Idling away your time, my darlings?'

Queen Isabel, who could move as quietly as a cat, stood in the doorway. Indeed, she looked rather feline with her high cheekbones and slanting green eyes. Her teeth were small and pointed, and her scarlet-tipped nails made little pools of blood against her white silk dress.

'We were talking, my lady mother,' Katharine said politely.

'And you couldn't bear to drag yourself away from your brother's conversation! What brilliant sallies of wit have you for me today, Charles dear? What amorous escapades have you to relate? Or perhaps you have some advice for me? My ministers can give me no constructive help, but then they lack your wisdom and experience.'

'We thought we might go down to the tiltyard,' Katharine said quickly.

Isabel's bright, amused glance strayed to her daughter.

'Do you wish to applaud your brother's consummate skill, my love? What a devoted family we are to be sure! Very well, let us go down together.'

She held out her narrow hands, smiling through shut teeth.

Was there ever a time, Charles wondered, when she was young and sweet and spoke without meaning to wound? Or was she born hard and shining and cruel, with malice in every glance and spite in every word she utters? Did she satisfy her lovers when she lay in their arms or did she drain them of everything they had to give, and give nothing in return?

As they walked with linked arms down the corridor, there was a bustle of retainers within the hall and a shambling figure appeared on the threshold. Bowing before his father, Charles felt the familiar emotions of repugnance and pity. The King's fur robe was tattered and mudstained, although his fingers gleamed with jewels. There were foodstains down his surcoat and his breath was sour.

'Where are you running off to, hey? Are you trying to escape? There is no escape, you know, unless one flies right out of the world. I think I might do that one day. *That* would cause a sensation! Where are you going?'

'To the tiltyard, Sire.'

'Splendid idea, splendid!' the King approved heartily. 'Young fellows, exercising in the fresh air! Comfits and wine to follow, hey?'

He seized Charles's arm and hung to it tightly. Isabel and

Katharine had moved away, with the smoothness of long practice, so that the boy was forced to accept the weight of the older man as the King leaned, chuckling and grimacing.

'The English ambassador was here this morning,' he confided, as they emerged into the bright sunshine where several gallants were having a desultory game of tilting at the ring. 'They don't tell me of these matters, but I find out things. Harry of England wants to make a treaty. There now, what do you think of that? A treaty that will give him the throne of France, no doubt! Well, he tried to claim this Kingdom once before, and I gave him an answer. I sent him a box of tennis-balls.'

'I know, Father.'

'Oh, have I told you before? Never mind, it's a good story. Shall we sit here? Why are those fools bowing?'

'Because you are the King, Father.'

'So I am! So I am! And you are—who are you? I know the face, but the name escapes me!'

'I am Charles, your son.'

'Dear me! I thought Charles was a little boy. But then time goes faster now. The angel of the hours has wound up all the clocks too tightly, and God hasn't noticed yet. Who did you say you were?'

'I am Charles, your son!'

He had not meant to speak so loudly, but his voice had shrilled out into a brief silence, and in the pause that followed his words he heard his mother laughing.

Then she turned her head and called, mockingly, 'Come and take your place among the young blood of the court then. I am sure they will find a quiet mount for you!'

Flushing darkly, aware of the stifled titters, he walked between the stands to the barrier and seized the bridle of the first horse he saw.

'Baretta is in a mettlesome temper today,' murmured Jean Dunois, coming up and pretending to tighten a stirrup.

'It matters not!'

20

'It matters if you fall and break your neck.'

'It's *my* neck,' Charles muttered, resentfully.

The older boy shrugged. 'Suit yourself, cousin. But don't tense in the saddle, then you're less likely to break a bone when you hit the ground.'

Dunois swung gracefully back to his own high-spirited white stallion and cantered to the further end of the yard, where his squire waited with lance and buckler.

Now he will try to make me win, Charles thought. He will swerve at the last moment and lose his balance and nobody will be deceived. Jean Dunois has many skills, but acting is not among them.

Gloomily he allowed himself to be fastened into the padded breastplate and helmet and winced inwardly as he glanced down at his spindly legs.

The herald raised the trumpet. His mother and sister were leaning forward as if they willed him to lose; the King had lost interest in the proceedings and was eating some daisies that grew in a clump by his chair; the sun glinted on the crisp turf and blunted weapons.

Then a high clear note sounded, and he was cantering towards Dunois. As Charles half-rose in the saddle, with the lance heavy in his palm, Baretta reared. Charles gripped the pommel desperately, but the lance in his hand twisted and there was a sickening crush as the heavy wood crashed across the open visor of his opponent. Dunois went down like a stone, and Charles, loosing his grip in horror, somer-saulted over the pommel and sprawled across his cousin in most unprincely style.

Queen Isabel cried out in excitement. 'Are they killed? Are they killed?'

Charles, feeling sick and dizzy raised himself cautiously, as Dunois sat up and gingerly felt his nose from which blood was streaming.

'You were supposed to unseat me,' he said mildly. 'Not knock my teeth in.'

'Are you badly hurt?'

'My nose is broken. I felt the bone crunch.'

The attendants were fussing around them and somebody was calling for the surgeon. Dunois got up and steadied himself against his squire's shoulder. He grinned cheerfully at the still-trembling Dauphin.

'No great harm done, but I shall have two magnificent black eyes by tonight. The ladies won't be too pleased.'

'Nonsense, you silly boy. They will all want to mother you,' Isabel said lightly.

She had strolled up to the agitated little group and stood, smiling and composed.

'With blood all over me, Madam!'

'Blood can be exciting.'

The Queen put up a slender finger to the boy's cheek, then licked her finger delicately while her darkened lashes fluttered.

Charles felt his stomach heave with disgust and misery.

'I cannot understand how you can be so clumsy,' Isabel said, over her shoulder. 'Your father was such a splendid horseman.'

'I thought the King disliked riding.'

'Oh, the King! Oh, indeed, the *King*!' Her voice trailed into laughter as if she had not been thinking of her husband at all.

It was a favourite game of hers, to hint that Charles was not the son of the King, but a by-blow from one of her lovers. But which lover?

Dunois, more mature than the Dauphin although less than a year separated them in age, sometimes wondered if he and Charles were closer in blood than cousins. Born out of wedlock to the King's brother, the Duke of Orleans, Jean Dunois was the favourite son of his father but not the only one. He knew that his father sometimes pleasured himself with Queen Isabel when the King was in a fit of madness; perhaps Charles had been the result of such an encounter.

Queen Isabel was staring at him as if she could read his thoughts, and he blushed hotly and moved closer to the

Dauphin as if to protect him.

'We should go inside out of the sun,' he hinted, speaking thickly over the congealing blood on his face.

'And the surgeon must dress your hurt! Forgive me cousin.'

Charles took Dunois by the arm and began to fuss.

But when the two boys, in shirt and hose relaxed, later in the garderobe, the Dauphin asked, abruptly, 'Do you believe I am truly the son of the King?'

'That's a strange question,' Dunois hedged.

'Not so strange. Many have asked it. My mother hints—'

'Your mother is a bitch,' said Dunois, with his usual frankness.

'She is the Queen,' Charles said gloomily.

'And one day you will be the King of France, and have more power than your mother ever dreamed about.'

The Dauphin's pale eyes brightened, then his head dropped again.

'By the time I am King, there will be no Kingdom for me to rule because Harry of England will have gobbled it all up.'

'Then I will win it all back for you!' Dunois sat up, a comic figure with bandaged nose and swollen eyes. 'When you are King, you must give me command of the army, and I will chase the goddams back into the sea.'

'And I will ride with you,' Charles said eagerly.

'You won't have time,' Dunois exclaimed, a trifle hastily. 'You will be too busy signing papers, and issuing proclamations, and making love to beautiful women. But I will win back France for you. I swear it!'

He looked oddly grave for a moment, and then his irrepressible grin flashed out.

'And by the time you are King,' he drawled, 'you will perhaps have saved up enough money to pay me for that suit!'

CHAPTER TWO

DOMREMY, JANUARY, 1420

THEY had once been respectable, prosperous folk who tended their flocks, bargained in the market place and minded their own business. Then the goddams had come, with their long bows and their hard eyes, and the villagers had fled into the forest, intending to return when the enemy moved on.

But when the enemy did move on, they left blackened, smoking ruins where once had been trim cottages and a village inn. And there were rumours that more goddams would follow, to destroy whatever had been rebuilt. So the community split up, some of its members to join relatives in safer areas, others to pile their remaining possessions on carts and travel slowly through the desolate provinces in search of work. But work was scarce and the winter was bitter. The very old and the very young died of cold and nobody regretted their passing for every death meant one fewer mouth to feed.

They were camped in the stubble fields of Domremy where they had been given permission to remain for one week. There was no employment in the district, but they might, said the village council of Domremy, cut timber from the forest and fish in the streams. Then they must move on, carefully skirting the borders of Burgundy, travelling in an endless circle through the divided land of France.

Time enough to think about that when the week was over. The villagers had once been accustomed to lay in supplies for the Christmas season, to knit shawls in readiness for the next baby, to put aside a few silver coins in case of accident or illness. But when the past, in the shape of home and farm, was destroyed, there seemed no point in preparing for the future. Now they lived from day to day, and sometimes from hour to hour, without thinking, because thought induced awareness and awareness brought pain.

Simon huddled closer to the side of the canvas tent and shivered. He would have liked to move to the fire in the centre of the encampment and take his place with the rest of the family. They would have made room for him, but it would have been in the consciously hearty manner that reminded him that he was no blood-kin to them but merely a foundling they had taken out of charity.

He had been ten years old when the Alains had first seen him, and they had given him food and a bed and expressed no surprise when he was still there the next morning. There were already eight children in the farmhouse and an extra one made no difference. Jacques Alain had ascertained from the child that he had no relatives and had run away from his last master who beat him cruelly, and there the matter had been left. The weals on Simon's back healed and he put on weight and grew taller as he followed Jacques about the farm, learning how to plough and sow and reap the corn.

But he never felt himself to be a true Alain, for Jacques, who cuffed his own sons indiscriminately, never raised a hand to him, and if there was an extra piece of bacon in the bowl, Madame would urge, 'Eat it up, Simon. You need some flesh on your bones.'

After the village had been destroyed, the Alains had taken Simon with them, calling out, 'Make room! Come and take your seat, boy. Don't hang behind.'

But hope died during the months of wandering. The food was still evenly divided, and Jacques sometimes gave up his own share to the children and swore he needed to lose some of his excess fat, but his kindness lay like a stone on Simon's heart.

Tonight there had been no supper for any of them, and Simon was almost pleased because he was spared the guilt of having to eat his share. But there was the next day to face and his courage failed him. It would be better to creep away in the darkness, and pray that none of the family would have strength or desire to follow.

Yet his legs refused to obey his will, but stayed bent against the chilly ground. At sixteen one needs regular meals and Simon knew that if he did not go at once, he would lack the energy for the effort.

Slowly he pulled himself upright and crept away, afraid lest the snapping of a twig betray his intentions. He did not look back to the closed circle of Alains about the fire, but he dreaded to hear the farmer's grimly cheerful tones, bidding him to join them, reminding him he was not one of them.

He moved more quickly when he had forded the stream, but kept to the deepest shadows in case somebody recognized him as one of the refugee camp and chased him away.

When he was almost at the end of the street a dog barked, so suddenly that Simon cringed against the wall. For a brief period during his childhood, he had been reduced to stealing in order to keep alive, and he had a souvenir of those times in the shape of a scar running down the calf of his leg where a dog had sprung at him.

The barking died away and there was silence again; for the citizens of Domremy rose and retired early as did most country-folk. Here and there a light still burned, but most of the shutters were closed.

He was leaning against a solidly built little house, and he rested his cheek against the rough stone for an instant and closed his eyes. For the first time, Simon realized that he had turned his back on the people who had befriended him. For six years he had never had to worry where his next meal was coming from or where he would sleep when night fell. He had lost the habit of looking after himself and he was bewildered and afraid.

He slid around the corner of the building and looked through open shutters into a warmly lit room, with some people sitting around the central hearth and talking in animated fashion. They were intent on their conversation, and

26

the woman stirring something in the pot on the fire had her back to the window.

Simon knew that he ought to duck down out of sight but something stronger than caution, an instinct compounded of pleasure and pain, held him motionless. Then a little girl in a red dress, looked up from the pile of skins on which she was sitting, and stared directly at him. Her mouth opened in surprise, but she remained silent. He moved away, stubbing his toe painfully on the cobbles and feeling tears spring up. When he was a safe distance from the house, he leaned against a tree and wept. He told himself that he was crying because his foot hurt, but in his mind was the picture of the smoky, firelit, room with its comfortably sprawling occupants.

'Boy, why are you crying?'

It was the girl in the red dress, staring at him from a little distance.

'I was not crying!'

Angrily he rubbed his eyes and nose on his sleeve.

'You *are* crying,' she contradicted, 'and you are going to cry again in a moment.'

'I have no home and nowhere to go, and no hope of work,' he said, and wondered why he bothered to explain matters to a child.

'Are you from the camp? Did the goddams burn down your village?'

He nodded and she came nearer to him; her face was a white disc in the gloom and there was sympathy in her voice.

'I have nowhere to go,' he repeated.

'Is that why you cry?'

'Isn't it reason enough?' he asked, crossly.

'If you have nowhere in particular to go,' she said, quaintly, 'then you can go anywhere in the world.'

'I need work. Can you offer me work?'

She shook her head. 'There's no work in the village at this end of the year. My father used to hire a man to help with the lambing, but my brothers are big enough to do most of the heavy work now.'

'Then I shall starve.'

He spoke with conscious self-pity hoping for more sympathy, but when she next spoke she sounded almost accusing.

'You need not starve. Why don't you go and fight the goddams?'

'All by myself?'

'Go to Vaucouleurs. The Governor has a great many soldiers there but he needs more to help him fight.'

'I don't know how to use a sword.'

'Oh, it's quite easy,' she assured him gravely. 'You hold a sword by the handle and run upon your enemy and split him through, so!'

'Unless he runs me through first!'

'Oh, if you are a *coward*!'

He was nettled by the contempt in her tone. 'Where is this Vaucouleurs?'

'Not very far. In that direction!' She waved her hand vaguely in a semi-circle.

'And they need soldiers there?'

'They need soldiers everywhere. My brothers both want to go and fight but my father says they are needed on the farm.'

'And will they take me, and teach me how to use a sword, and pay me?'

'I'm sure they will.'

A door at the side of the house opened, and the woman who had been cooking over the fire, poked out her head. 'Joan! Joan!' she shouted crossly, 'will you come in the house this instant! How dare you wander about in the night air.'

'I'm coming, Mother!'

The little girl hesitated a moment, then darted forward and thrust something into Simon's hand. Then she pulled her scarf over her head and ran towards the open door.

Simon heard the sound of a smack and the woman's voice raised to a higher pitch.

'To leave the room without permission and breathe in the evil vapours of the night! I never knew such a wilful child. Go to your bed at once!'

The door closed with a bang and a moment later there was the rattle of shutters across the window.

Simon unclenched his fist, and peered at the lump of cheese the little girl had placed there. It was hard and smelt none too fresh, but he felt a great lightness of heart as he fingered it. The child had not screamed when she saw him spying from the window, but had slipped out quietly with the intention of helping him. She had given him the cheese in a fashion that bound them both together as conspirators, and she had risked punishment.

Simon bit into the rind and found it more palatable than he had expected. There was some water lying half-frozen in a hollow at the foot of the tree. He knelt down and, with difficulty, cupped a mouthful of the liquid and swallowed it.

Then he stood up again and took another bite of the cheese. If he walked swiftly, keeping to the main path but with eyes and ears open for any who could steal up behind him, he might reach the town of which the child had spoken.

Unconsciously, he had already reverted to the days when happiness was a mouthful of food and a road to travel, and when ambition went no further than the need to survive.

TROYES, JUNE, 1420

It had been a day that the people of Troyes would long remember. A day of colour and splendour, with bells pealing and red wine flowing from the conduits. If one drank enough of the free wine it was possible to forget that all this gaiety was due to the fact that Queen Isabel had made peace with the English.

It was an uneasy, shameful peace because, according to the terms of the treaty, the French throne would pass at the death of the King, not to the Dauphin, but to Henry V of England whose armies were grinding French pride into the dust. There was a sop to Gallic national feeling in the fact that when Harry of England came to the throne of France, he would already have a French Queen; it having been agreed that the Princess Katharine should marry him at once.

Hence the free wine and the flag-decked streets and the shouting, jostling cheering crowds. English and Burgundians swelled the ranks of spectators, and in the noise and excitement of the occasion the pickpockets had their most profitable day in years.

Shouldering his way through a group of housewives eagerly discussing the royal bride's silver head-dress, Giles sought a tavern where he could slake his thirst. It was worse than useless to wait one's turn for the free wine and beneath his dignity to grovel among the poorer citizens when he had money in his pouch. He usually had a well-filled purse these days, mainly because he had taken every advantage of the opportunities to fight provided during the long wars. Sir Atholl Beaumont was dead and his raiding party disbanded. Some of the men had returned to their homes and settled there, but Giles had no desire for a placid, rural existence. He had remained on the Continent, offering his fighting experience and his skill with the long bow to the highest bidders. He had even fought once with Italian and Burgundian mercenaries, but he had rejoined his own side before Agincourt, and it had never ceased to be a source of gratification to him that he had formed one of the long line of archers against which the French cavalry had splintered.

The treaty meant little beyond the chance to relax and see Troyes, and spend his money. He doubted if the peace would last for very long but even if it did there was always a war going on somewhere. He was not yet thirty, and apart from a slight twinge in his leg caused by an old wound, his health and vigour were unimpaired. Perhaps when he was too old to draw his bow smoothly he would go home again.

The tavern was below street-level and none too clean, but he found a seat and paid for a tankard of Rhenish without complaint, although he was aware he had been grossly over-charged.

As he drank, his eyes roved about the dark interior. He wanted a woman, but was quite prepared to wait for a while until a young and passably pretty one came along. Two bawds in the corner of the room smiled in his direction, but one had the ravages of smallpox on her face, and the other had red hair and reminded him of the trollop who had given him a dose of the French disease three years before.

He drained the tankard and went up again into the narrow street. If nobody took his fancy during the next few minutes he would go back to his lodgings and split a keg of wine with his comrades, if they had returned.

Then he saw the brilliant yellow hair and blue eyes of a young girl who stood watching him. She was too thin for his tastes, with the wolfish, avid look of a typical street urchin but then she smiled at him, cocking her head impudently and beckoning. He went over and took her hand, bending over and noticing, with a shock of pleased surprise, that her hair smelled clean and fresh, and her skin was smooth. She pressed his hand against her pointed breasts and pouted at him. Her heart was beating very fast, with excitement he thought for it never crossed his mind that she might be nervous.

'Bertha,' she said, indicating herself.

'Giles,' he said, politely; and she echoed the name, slurring it on her tongue.

She would do very well, he thought, although she was

not above thirteen or fourteen. Then she untied the lace of her bodice and pulled his hand closer, and his mind stopped speculating about her as the slow fire rose up in his loins.

When he woke much later, he expected to find his wallet gone and the girl with it, but she was still lying beside him, with her hair spread about her face. She had brought him to her home, he supposed, and he admitted that it was bare but tidy, with the floor swept and sacking pinned neatly across the doorway and the window.

It was pleasant to lie beside her, watching the colour of her hair vary from gold to bronze as the light faded. He had just decided that he would pay her twice what she asked, when the sacking was pushed aside and a man strode in.

The girl stirred and woke as quickly as a child wakes. When she saw the newcomer she broke into a torrent of what sounded like abuse, screeching and spitting. The man interrupted her tirade by knocking her two or three times across the head with the back of his hand, and she subsided weeping.

Giles swore under his breath and fumbled for some coins, but when he threw them on the mattress, the man grabbed them and held out his hand for more. The girl stopped crying and sat up, with an interested expression on her face.

Giles measured the distance between his opponent and himself with a practised eye. This was not the first time his financial arrangements with a woman had been interrupted when her bully arrived and demanded more. The notion of paying her double was thrust aside, for Giles who was generally considered to be generous had no intention of submitting to intimidation.

This pimp was fairly typical of his kind, big but thick about the waist, with an unhealthy pallor. He appeared to be unarmed, but his hand hung down near his belt and Giles was well-aware that somewhere a knife lay concealed.

He shrugged and opened his pouch again, watching from

the corner of his eye for the precise moment when the other man relaxed his stance. Then he flung the contents of the pouch in the face of the bully and sprang across the space between.

The other fell backwards on the stone floor. There was a sharp crack, and then as Giles picked himself up, the sound of the girl's delighted clapping.

'Goddam it!'

Giles stared down at the motionless figure, noting the trickle of blood from the ear and the half-open eyes. On a dozen other occasions the fellow would merely have been knocked out; but this one had to have a skull that cracked like an egg. He sat back on his heels, biting his lip thoughtfully.

Bertha's delight was fading. She had no pity for the man who lay dead or dying on the floor. Her father had never treated her well. As a little girl she had cringed from his blows, and it had been a relief when she grew out of childhood because then, provided she brought back sufficient money for his daily ration of wine, he stopped hitting her. She even enjoyed her trade because she was young and pretty and could pick and choose her clients, avoiding the diseased and perverted.

There had been times when she dreamed of loving one man, not for money, but because he was good to be near. One or two youths, seeing her in the streets, looked as if they would have liked to know her better, but when she smiled invitingly they recognized the tricks of the trade that came to her almost automatically, and went off to find a decent girl for a sweetheart.

She watched the Englishman carefully, knowing he had not meant to kill, and sensing also that he intended to leave her. She would have to explain what had happened and they might not believe her. They might accuse her of having pushed her father during an argument over payment.

She wondered if she might appeal to the Beggars for

help. In the cities the underworld was a finely organized society, its members bound by rules and codes as strict as any imposed by the law. But the King of the Beggars exacted body and soul from the members of his Kingdom, and if Bertha obtained protection from such a quarter, payment would be extracted for the rest of her life.

Then her heart lifted, because the Englishman was cramming the money back into the pouch and handing it to her. Obviously he trusted her and intended to take her with him. She would not have to appeal to the Beggars for help, or face the authorities alone.

Giles, having given her the pouch, left the wooden shack. Behind him, Bertha pattered obediently, wishing he would have waited a moment longer so that she could collect her few bits and pieces before they left; but he was evidently anxious to be gone, and she followed, unquestioning.

Giles, glancing back and seeing her, cursed, for the first time, his mental laziness that had prevented him from learning any French. Obviously, the foolish doxy considered they were now travelling companions, partners-in-crime. He raised his hand with the intention of waving her back, and she immediately trotted up to him and smiled happily. If she had possessed a tail, he thought gloomily, she would have wagged it.

He wondered if she would shout and make a scene if he did send her away. The streets were still crowded, and now that the main festivities were over, most people were settling down to serious drinking. Giles decided it would be wiser to leave the city behind before he tried to get rid of his unwanted companion. She was walking by his side with the top of her yellow head brushing his sleeve. But he no longer felt any attraction towards the girl once his desire was satisfied.

Bertha's feet were rubbed raw in her thin sandals by the time they had left the streets and squares of the city behind and come into the open countryside, with its patches of marsh land and edges of dark forest. She was thankful when Giles sat down in the shadow of a hedge and, tilting his cap over his eyes, apparently fell asleep at once.

She had never slept in the open before, nor walked so far beyond the city, but the Englishman's steady breathing reassured her. She curled up beside him and fell asleep as speedily as a puppy, with her shallow little mind empty of dreams.

The sun, striking through cloud, disturbed her. She rolled away, rubbing her eyes and yawning. Then she realized that the field was empty, that she lay alone under the hedge, and that, although the pouch had gone, four gold coins glinted near her hand.

For a moment she was so disappointed that she started to cry. The Englishman had never intended to take her with him at all. He had brought her to this lonely place and left her while she slept.

She tucked the coins into the pocket sewn within her skirt and wiped her eyes angrily. By now the English archer would be far away, and she dare not return home because they might have discovered her father's body.

She started to walk aimlessly along the hedge, scuffing the turf with her toes. Her feet were still sore and she was beginning to feel extremely hungry.

The soldier, riding out into the country to clear his head after the previous night's drinking, swerved to avoid a tree-stump and shouted a greeting.

Bertha waited until his horse's head almost touched her shoulder, then she looked up and smiled.

He was an unshaven, foolish-looking fellow who might have a soft heart, so she said nothing but gazed up at him, forcing tears into her blue eyes and shaking her curls artlessly.

He leaned from the saddle and hoisted her effortlessly behind him. She put her arms round his waist and smiled again. He had greeted her in French but his accent was Burgundian, and she had heard that nearly a thousand Burgundians were camped on the other side of the river. Surely, among a thousand men, there would be one willing to give her his protection!

TROYES, JUNE, 1420

Henry, King of England and heir-apparent to the throne of France, stood by the open window and stretched luxuriously. In the high canopied bed, Katharine snuggled further down between the quilts and eyed him with sly appreciation.

This English husband was, she decided, a fine man. He was not very tall nor strikingly handsome, but he radiated vitality from the top of his crisp red-gold head to his well-muscled legs. Even his skin had a faint golden sheen, and when he laughed he threw back his head, showing a full set of excellent teeth.

Katharine decided she was indeed fortunate. Henry might so easily have been old and ugly, or even half-witted. When royal marriages were arranged, the wishes of the bride were seldom considered. And Katharine had not wanted to marry the English King. She had thought of him as a barbarian and shuddered, imagining thick hands and insatiable lips. Her mother, guessing her thought, had laughed.

'They say the English King is experienced in matters of love. I hope you will not disappoint him, for if you do you are no daughter of mine.'

'Will you then disown me as you have disowned Charles?' Katharine asked, pertly.

Isabel took the girl's face between her hands, pressing back the skin until the bones stood out sharply.

'We must all make sacrifices for reasons of state,' she said.

'And I must marry for reasons of state,' Katharine said, forlornly.

'So that you may provide an heir to follow your husband upon the twin thrones.'

'And my brother, Charles?'

'Is a fool and a simpleton! If he ever came to the throne of France he would not hold it above a twelvemonth. So, cease bleating about your brother!'

Isabel had whirled away, leaving faint blue marks on Katharine's cheeks.

The princess had felt sick and afraid. Her mother was right, of course, for Isabel had more political sense than most men. The wars had continued for so long and it was impossible for France to win, so a treaty sealed by a marriage made good sense. But what of Charles? Katharine agreed that he was foolish and irresolute, but what chance had he ever been given to develop more Kingly qualities? What chance had any of them ever had, with an insane father and a mother who lusted after men and power?

Katharine despised Charles but she was fond of him, too fond to relish the prospect of being married to the man who now took his place in the succession. She had even had the ridiculous idea of refusing to go through with the ceremony and of running away to join her brother at Chinon. They might raise an army together, drive out the English and subdue the Burgundian faction, and bring an end to the quarrel once and for all.

Then her commonsense had reasserted itself. Even if she succeeded in evading the guards and finding her way to Chinon, the Dauphin would not help her to retain his promised throne. Anyway, girls were not allowed to lead armies or to ride into battle. They must stay quietly at home until their husbands were chosen for them, and then they must spend the rest of their lives having children.

She thought she might send a letter to Charles, explaining that she had been forced to consent to the match. But even if she wrote such a letter she knew of nobody who would deliver it.

Then they had brought in her wedding dress of white satin, sewn all over with pearls and in the excitement of trying it on, she had forgotten the Dauphin. There had been no time to think or even to feel afraid.

Queen Isabel was determined that the marriage would take place as speedily as possible, and the Court was in a ferment with dressmakers, cooks, tailors, grooms, and embroiderers rushing hither and thither among the excited officials while Isabel stormed and raged because her diamond bracelets had been mislaid.

By some miracle, everything was ready when the English contingent arrived. Peeping from her window, Katharine had lost count of the soldiers marching into the courtyard. All of them were heavily armed, and many of them wore full armour.

'He comes to his marriage as if he were riding to war!' Queen Isabel exclaimed, and her eyes glowed at the thought of her daughter's strong bridegroom.

Then, seizing Katharine's arm, she hurried her down to the great hall where the Court was assembled. Here the princess seated herself on a stool below the dais, and felt her heart bound with relief when her betrothed walked in, because the English King looked fresh and gay and very much master of the situation.

Had Katharine but known it, it had taken Henry more courage to walk in and claim his bride than to lead the first charge at Agincourt. He had been forced to bolster his nerve with a stiff dose of malmsey before he ordered the trumpeters to announce his approach.

The thought of marriage terrified the King. Sooner or later he knew that he must marry in order to provide heirs, but up to now he had successfully avoided the snares laid by eager princesses. Women were all very well in bed. There they were delightful creatures, but to be forced to live with one permanently! To have to endure nagging, or reproachful glances if one was unfaithful! Or to be mated with a cow-faced wench for the sake of policy!

Henry had been appalled when he learned that the French King would not sign the treaty acknowledging him as heir unless he agreed to marry the Princess Katharine.

'Fine parents-in-law you're gaining!' teased Warwick. 'A man who is insane three-quarters of the time, and a woman who has openly declared her son to be a bastard, thus stigmatizing her husband as cuckold and herself as whore!'

Henry's worst fears had been confirmed as he stood before the dais and looked up at the yellow-faced monarch with the lolling head, and the woman in gold tissue whose eyes stripped him of his fine doublet, so that he had the crazy notion that he was standing naked in the great hall.

'Henry of England, we greet Your Grace and bid you welcome to our humble Court.'

The Queen had risen and came down to meet him, extending her hand to be kissed, while her narrow eyes beneath their plucked brows sparkled at him.

If only we could send away all these others and be alone together, said the Queen's eyes, then I would show you the full extent of Gallic hospitality.

Aloud, she said, 'Will you not sit with us upon the dais? It would signify the new friendship between our countries. The King has waited so long for this day.'

Glancing at King Charles, Henry doubted it. The French monarch was beginning to fidget, and to enquire loudly why supper wasn't ready.

'You speak our tongue so fluently,' Isabel flattered, 'Katharine will be relieved for her command of the English language is not as far advanced as I could wish. Indeed, she is very young for her years in other ways.'

Too young for an experienced man of the world like yourself, said the eyes. I am not so very many years older than you, and in the darkness you would not even remember that.

'I am longing to meet my sweet bride,' Henry said, politely, drawing away slightly because the perfume used by the Queen had a sickly, cloying aroma.

Isabel's face hardened, but she replied at once. 'Then we

must satisfy your longing. Katharine, make your curtsey!'

The slender girl in white, rose from her stool and bowed submissively to her knees. Henry's heart sank into his elegant boots, as he took in the thin hips and small breasts and delicate bones of the princess.

She was really quite lovely, one part of his mind argued. Her features were fine despite an overlong nose, and her eyes were like dark almonds. Her skin was white as milk, and her attitude was graceful.

The other part of his mind told him firmly that she did not look strong enough for child-bearing, and that there was about her an unmistakably virginal air.

Henry, who avoided virgins and preferred to take his pleasures with lusty girls whose feelings it was unnecessary to consider, decided that he was indeed making a great sacrifice for the sake of a throne.

He went through the official wedding ceremony on the following day in the same pessimistic spirit. The princess looked more remote and fragile than ever, and her hand trembled as he slid the gold ring on to her finger. She had spoken scarcely a word during the banquet, and when he had tried to make conversation those around fell silent so that his voice boomed out.

Henry was not a sensitive man, but he blushed with temper and embarrassment when he saw the other guests smiling behind their hands. And it took all of his self-control not to reach for his dagger when King Charles, who had behaved remarkably well until that moment, suddenly remarked, 'The goddam has the sort of table-manners one might expect.'

He was hastily coaxed into silence, and Isabel leaned across and refilled Henry's goblet, smiling up at him through her curled lashes.

Damn them all, Henry swore. Who cared for the opinions of a lot of perfumed, perverted foreigners? He was interested only in formal recognition as the future King of France. Was he not descended from the great

William of Normandy who had invaded England and had the sense to settle down there? Ever since that time the Kings of England had styled themselves also as Kings of France, and these recent campaigns had won back for Henry nearly all the original English possessions in France. The glory and the credit of these military conquests went to England, and by England Henry meant himself.

'I wonder where Charles is,' the French King said loudly. 'He usually comes to all the celebrations.'

'You forget, Sire,' Queen Isabel said, 'that the Dauphin is at his castle of Chinon. Your new heir sits with us now.'

'The goddam?'

'The King of England; and one day he will be King of France,' Isabel said sharply.

'Not for a long time, please God,' Henry said briskly.

Charles fixed him with disconcertingly sane eyes and waved a spoon in rebuke.

'Don't lie, my fine fellow. You can't wait to sit where I'm sitting. After all, your own father hurried his cousin, Richard Plantagenet into his grave so that he could take the English throne!'

There was a babble of agitated chatter as everybody began talking at once.

'We will have to put him away again soon,' Isabel said. 'He grows more frenzied.'

Or more sincere, Henry thought. He wondered why people should imagine he minded the fact that his father had come to the throne over the murdered corpse of Richard the Second. Yet his father had regretted the murder and done public penance for it. Warwick had asked Henry once if he undertook so many foreign campaigns because he wanted to prove what a splendid right he had to be King; but Henry, never analytical, had stared at him in bewilderment.

The interminable banquet ended. The bedding ceremony followed, with King Charles dissolving into tears, the English lords making sly jokes about French girls, and Queen

Isabel leaning so low to snuff the candles that her breasts were completely exposed.

Then he was alone with the almond-eyed girl in the bed hung with tapestry and surmounted by fleur-de-lys twining around the leopards of England.

Now, in the high sun of a new day, Henry stretched and yawned and wondered why he had been so anxious. Virginal Katharine certainly was, but he should have remembered she was her mother's daughter. Her sensuality had leapt to meet his own, and her fragile child's body had been unexpectedly sweet and strong.

I will take her back to England, thought Henry, and ensure that she is pregnant before I return to France and make my conquest completely certain.

He turned and smiled at her, and she wrinkled her nose at him so delightfully that he was inspired to seek their bed again.

CHAPTER THREE

LONDON, NOVEMBER, 1422

THE people stood in silence with bared heads, paying no heed to the flurries of bitter wind sweeping up from the river. There were veterans of the wars, paying tribute to the King who had led them to victory and cared about them. There were women, remembering with tears how the bells had rung out joyfully eleven months before to announce the birth of an heir to the throne. Now the bells tolled, dull and mournful, and the excited cheers had turned to the slow beating of drums.

Children were lifted shoulder-high so that they could see the black hearse, drawn by black horses, covered with the leopards of England. Above the coffin stood the huge leather effigy of the late King, clad in the royal robes with a sceptre in the right hand and a golden apple in the left. Behind the carriage rode the great noblemen of the land.

There were the King's brothers, John of Bedford and Humphrey of Gloucester, managing even at this solemn moment to keep their horses well apart and glare at each other over the intervening space. Here came the Earl of Warwick, his cloak sewn with black pearls, and Henry Beaufort, bishop of Winchester, with his heavy face tight with grief. King James of Scotland rode alone, muffled in sables.

Now came the clergy, bearing tapers and dressed in white; and the grey-clad yeomen, carrying their bows behind Henry's coffin as they had carried them behind him at Agincourt, Caen, Falaise, Rouen, Montereau and Melun.

So many campaigns, and some in bitter weather, when the horses fell into the mud and stifled there, and men cried aloud with the pain of frozen fingers.

The Queen's carriage was passing now and the crowds

stood on tiptoe to catch a glimpse of the slender girl, veiled in black. How they had cheered when Henry brought home his French bride! Few cared that her father was insane and her mother a bawd. She was a trophy of war; and the King had loved her well and taken her back with him to France when the troubles there broke out again.

The crowds had stood often in the streets to watch their King ride back from war. There were those who had seen him as a youth roistering with his friends in the taverns of the city; but he had given up his riotous living when he came to the throne and turned his energies to conquest. What did it matter if taxes were high and the roads of England ill-mended? Had he not brought under English control lands that belonged to England by hereditary right? Who, stretching to see that gallant figure in armour, had not rejoiced because the King was home again, having inflicted a further humiliation upon the French?

This was the last homecoming, and the saddest. Henry V had not fallen in battle for no Frenchman was worthy to strike such a blow, but had died of dysentery. There was not a soldier who had not at some time felt the painful stomach cramps and the unhappy necessity of squatting on the ground amid the flying cannon balls. And Harry of England had fallen victim to the soldier's hazard. In life he had led his men, sharing their food and walking among them, and in dying he shared their common discomfort.

So the crowds stood in silent tribute, and within her carriage the widowed Katharine veiled her face and thought bitter thoughts.

The King loved me, and I loved him, and bore him a fair son. Yet he made no provision for me when he lay dying. There was time for him to settle all his affairs, but he never mentioned me. He knew that he would not recover, but he never sent for me. Was I mistaken after all and did he look upon me merely as a bargain in a treaty? Yet he called me 'sweet Katharine' and kept me by his side, and in the long nights we whispered together.

She lifted her veil to dab her eyes, remembering how proud he had been when young Henry was born. The baby was strong and beautiful but Katharine would be allowed no part in the rearing of him. The tiny King was to be brought up by his uncles, Bedford and Gloucester, and God help the poor mite! thought Katharine, for they will fight over him as dogs fight over a piece of meat and not notice that they have pulled the titbit to pieces between them.

Her son was an important child, soon to be crowned as King Henry VI of England, and also King of France for poor mad King Charles had died, raving, the previous month. Katharine shivered, wondering if the child would be allowed to claim his inheritance peacefully. A party of loyal supporters had gathered around her brother who might be urged to fight for the throne. The only hope lay in an Anglo-Burgundian alliance, and Charles might be kept quiet then with the gift of a few castles.

I will have no voice in any future struggle, thought Katharine. I dare not return to France lest my brother's faction seize me, and I would not willingly live with my mother again. But if I stay in England, where will I live? A widow does not flaunt herself in public, and they will not allow me to share my son's household.

The carriage had stopped before the great doors of Westminster Abbey, and a gentleman waited to hand her down.

She recognized him vaguely as a member of the household, and wondered why he looked so familiar. Then she remembered that the King had sent for him one evening and bade him entertain them by singing and playing upon the harp. What was it that Henry had said? 'This is Owen Tudor, my love, who sings like an angel and fights like a devil'. Owen Tudor! That was his name, and he had come from Wales. Katharine recalled that he had amused them by reciting something in a strange tongue. His eyes had glowed, and when he played the harp, his long fingers caressed the strings.

When the funeral is over, Katharine decided, I might

ask the Council to allow me to retire somewhere quiet, with a few members of my household. Perhaps I could travel to Wales, and live a peaceful rural existence there, away from courts and quarrels and the ambitions of great men.

DOMREMY, JULY, 1426

The tiny white chapel in the heart of the woods was deserted, and the trees themselves seemed to drowse in the hot sunshine. Underfoot the turf was browned by the heat and the stream trickled thinly over round pebbles.

Further down the valley sheep grazed placidly while their youthful guardians sat in the comparative shade of the hedge and drank their ration of well-watered wine. Four of them sat, as usual, in a tight closed circle, talking and laughing in a private, animated way. These four were always together, so that if one saw Hauviette or Joan, one automatically looked around for Michel or Jean. It had been natural to bracket their names together, ever since they had made their first communions.

Michel and Jean were both sixteen and considered themselves experienced men of the world. Indeed, Michel regularly drove his father's cattle to market at Greux and Vaucouleurs, and usually brought back a ribbon or a bit of lace for Joan.

At first he had given the presents to Joan because Hauviette needed no fancy trinkets to set off her chestnut curls and wide grey eyes. But he was becoming conscious of the fact that Joan's smiling words of gratitude meant more than Hauviette's delighted squeals.

The two girls were sitting close together, plaiting daisies into a crown. Joan's long brown hands worked smoothly and skilfully, inducing, in the boy who watched, a pleasant inertia. Her head, with its glossy braid of black hair, was bent over the pile of blossoms in her skirt. Her underlip was caught between her teeth and she breathed heavily in concentration.

Hauviette snagged her nail suddenly in a piece of stem and crossly pushed her share of the flowers aside.

'I'm bored!' she complained. 'Can't any of you think of anything interesting to do?'

'We're supposed to guard the animals,' Jean Waterin pointed out.

'Guard them from what? There hasn't been a raid in months!'

'They might stray,' Jean said, mildly.

'They haven't the energy to walk more than a yard,' Hauviette said impatiently.

'What do you want to do?' Joan asked, balancing the finished wreath between her hands and studying it critically.

'We could go to the Bois Chenu,' Hauviette said, 'and look for fairy-rings on the grass.'

'You still don't believe all that nonsense!' Jean exclaimed.

'Madame Aubry believes in fairies,' Hauviette said, indignantly. 'She saw fairies once, dancing around the big oak tree in the Bois Chenu. She saw them with her own eyes, and she's the Mayor's wife so her word must count for something!'

'We could go over to Greux. That old woman who keeps pigs there—you know, the smelly one—well, she has a mandrake.'

'Have you seen it, Michel?' Joan asked.

'No, but Estellin has seen it. He says she talks to it as if it were a baby.'

'Is it true that mandrakes scream when they're pulled out of the ground?' Hauviette asked in a low voice.

'I know you can work spells with mandrakes,' Jean countered.

'How do you know? Have you ever worked a spell?' Joan asked scornfully.

47

'Well, no, but mandrakes are evil. Only witches use them.'

'Then we ought not to want to see it,' Joan said, folding her lips primly.

'Well, what shall we do?'

'Let's run races and the winner will get the daisy crown.'

'Boys can't wear flowers in their hair,' Hauviette giggled. 'And it's too hot to run about.'

'Some exercise will do you good. If you sit about all day you'll grow as fat as old Beatrice.' Joan jumped up eagerly, tired of being still. 'And if the boys win, they can give the flowers to the girl of their choice!'

'That sounds fair,' Jean said, with his eyes on Hauviette's pretty face.

Joan was already running to the further end of the meadow, with her red skirts swirling about her bare ankles.

'We'll give you a start!' Michel shouted, but she made a face at him impishly.

'If I started behind you,' she called, 'I'd still reach the winning post first.'

'To the big hawthorn and back to the beech tree,' Jean cried.

A few of the younger children hurried to join the game, and the field echoed with laughter and voices.

'Joan, I see you flying above the ground!' one small girl cried excitedly, watching Joan's feet flash across the turf.

Joan won by a length and flung herself, panting, against the bank.

'Put on the crown. You won it fairly.' Michel had come breathlessly up to her, and held out the garland.

'I don't want it. It's wilting already.'

She had lost interest in the prize, and Michel's face clouded a little.

He and Joan were constant companions, but he some-times had the odd notion that she looked at him without seeing him. She was growing away from the others and it was troubling because of late he had begun to watch her

48

when she was not aware of it.

She was not aware of him now, but sat, staring into space, with a listening expression on her face. He put out his hand to touch her shoulder, but she got up and moved, striding away from him through a gap in the hedge.

'Where is Joan going?' Hauviette asked.

'Off by herself somewhere.' Michel shrugged and started to pull the browning petals of the daisies apart.

'She might have waited,' Hauviette said, but being a good-humoured child she quickly forgot her resentment, and coaxed the two boys to go back with her to the village where Madame Estellin might be flattered into giving them sugar-cakes.

Joan had gone in the opposite direction, hurrying across the fields and down the steep path to the edge of the wood. She had no clear idea of where or why she was going. She knew only that the usual compulsion had gripped her and that the voices were getting louder.

She had first heard the voices two years previously when she was weeding the garden. Her hands were gritty with dirt and the edge of her skirt was muddy for it had rained the previous day and was still overcast and gloomy. She felt warmth on the nape of her neck and raised her face, but the sun still sulked behind its clouds although the garden was full of light. She passed her hand across her eyes and shook her head, and then a voice had spoken, calling her by name and telling her not to be afraid.

It had all lasted only a few seconds, then the garden was gloomy again with drops of rain splashing on her hand. But after that she heard the voices often. Sometimes there were two or three together, whispering in her head. At other times, a single voice spoke to her clearly, so clearly that she would spin about to catch a glimpse of the speaker but see nothing except a flash of light. The voices were gentle but often spoke so quickly that it was difficult to understand the words. At other times, she heard them quite plainly, telling her to be good because there was great work for her to perform.

When other people were around, it had worried her lest they be frightened by the voices but she quickly realized that the others heard nothing. So she never spoke of these things for she had no wish to be dosed with Zabillet's home-made physic or spanked for telling lies.

Sometimes she felt guilty when Michel nudged her sharply and asked her if she had heard a word he was saying, and when Hauviette cried because Joan had run off by herself into the fields, drawn there by the urgency of the voices. But when she finally stood in the empty meadow, nothing ever happened. The grasses stirred in the breeze; the cows stared at her incuriously; the voices in her head died away; she was completely alone although she sensed that she was being watched; by whom or by what she didn't know save that she felt no fear.

She was in the forest now, standing outside the little whitewashed chapel of Bermont. The sun struck a white glare from the pointed roof of the shrine and through the low doorway she could see the statue of the Holy Virgin, clumsily and lovingly carved by some long-forgotten hermit.

Disappointment gripped her. This was going to be like the other times, when she rushed eagerly towards something that never happened. She ought to return to her friends and apologize for leaving them so abruptly.

Yet she stayed where she was, breathing in the scent of lilies, though none grew within sight. The trees were obscured by a mist of gold so bright and soft that she had the feeling one might trickle the gold through one's fingers or use it as a scarf.

Then, without any sense of surprise, but with a surge of joy because this time the promise was fulfilled, she saw them smiling at her. Their crowns dazzled her gaze, their perfume drowned her senses, and as she sank slowly to her knees their familiar voices rose in greeting.

'But why must you rush off to Vaucouleurs at this time of all times?' Michel had protested.

'Why is this time so different?' Joan asked.

'I don't expect you to be interested,' Michel said loftily, 'but it's my birthday next week and my father has promised me that now I'm eighteen, he will pay me a regular wage for the work I do on the farm.'

'So?'

'So I planned to take you to the fair at Greux. We can drink wine and eat garlic sausage and watch the jugglers. Your parents would give you some time off, now that the lambing season is over.'

'Take Hauviette to the fair.'

'Jean is taking Hauviette, and anyway I want to be with you. I want to spend my first wages on you.'

'You ought to save them for your old age,' Joan said, provokingly.

'We may none of us have an old age,' Michel said with youthful pessimism, 'now that the goddams and the Burgundians have made an alliance. We could be invaded at any time. My father says the Dauphin will never capture his throne.'

'Your father is wrong. The throne of France will be saved.'

'By a virgin out of Lorraine? Yes, I've heard that old story too! Please, Joan, put off your visit for a while.'

'I can't! I have to go now.'

'Just to visit your cousins? Are you sure you haven't a lover at Vaucouleurs? You haven't, have you, Joan?'

'No, of course not.'

'Then stay at home. If you stay at home, I'll buy you a ring when we go to the fair.'

'I've got two rings already.' Joan held up her work-roughened hand where two bands gleamed incongruously. 'My brothers gave me one ring when I made my first Holy Communion, and my cousin brought me a ring when he came to stay last summer.'

'You know that's not what I meant!'

She was silent, biting her lip. Everybody took it for granted that she and Michel Lebuin would get married eventually. They had played together as children, had sat together watching the sheep, had knelt together at the altar to receive communion. The Lebuins were respectable and prosperous, and Michel was both strong and kind-hearted.

Until recently it would not have occurred to her to question the fact that their lives would move along the same path. Now she had been directed another way, and she could not reconcile old habits with her new dream.

'Please, Joan, you must know what I mean,' Michel was saying earnestly. 'You must know how I feel about you. Your parents expect it; my father has said that if I choose a wife he will give me land on which to build a cottage; and I never thought of choosing any other girl as wife.'

He broke off, catching her hand and squeezing it in an effort to convey his feelings. Joan let him hold it for a moment, then drew away and went on peeling carrots, with unnecessary vigour.

'Let me go to Vaucouleurs to see my cousins,' she said at last, 'and when I return, I'll give you my answer.'

He nodded, knowing from the firmness of her tone, that it was useless to badger her further.

As Michel went out, Jacques d'Arc came in from the yard where he had been sluicing his hands and face under the pump.

'Dreaming again, girl?' He poured himself a stoup of wine and drank thirstily.

'Michel was here,' she said, briefly.

'I saw him leave. When are you going to give the boy a definite answer?'

52

'So you know about—?'

'Everybody in Domremy wonders when they will get the chance to drink your wedding toast. You're past sixteen and it's time to settle down.'

'I asked him to wait.'

'Wait for what? Do you think a handsome gallant will come riding by and sweep you up into the saddle? Those are foolish dreams and you can't afford such foolishness. Michel won't wait for ever, and it's not as if you were beautiful. I'll provide you with a good dowry and a bit extra so that you can buy some pretty dresses, so come now.'

'I said I would let him know when I come back from Vaucouleurs.'

'And why you have to take it into your head to go off on a holiday!' Her father's lack of comprehension exploded into irritation. 'I'll not deny you're a good, obedient child but girls should stay close to their homes, not gallivant around the countryside. In these troubled times the roads are not safe, and I have had dreams.'

'Dreams, Father?'

'For months now, I have seen you in dreams, riding with soldiers. Hundreds of soldiers, and you in the middle of them! Only one type of woman joins the soldiers and we do not name such females in decent households. If I thought that you, my own daughter, were in danger of such a life of shame, I would rather see you dead at my feet! I would order your brothers to drown you in the well!'

'Why are you shouting so loudly?' Zabillet interrupted. 'I can hear you down at the byre.'

As usual she looked placid and cheerful. Joan envied her mother the quiet strength with which she dealt with every problem, and wondered if, when she herself had reached forty, she would face life so calmly.

'I don't like this trip to Vaucouleurs,' Jacques said, abruptly.

'Oh, come now, husband!' Zabillet put down the bucket she was carrying and folded her arms. 'Joan deserves a treat. She's still young enough to crave a little excitement, and God knows! we all grow old soon enough. My niece and her husband will see that she comes to no harm; and when she comes back, she will be the more ready to settle.'

So, it had been decided, and Jacquemin, grumbling over the inconvenience, drove his sister to their relatives at Burey-le-Petit, on the outskirts of Vaucouleurs.

Durand Lassois received Joan with the fussy kindness that distinguished him, and she lost no time in asking him for help.

'Take you to the Governor? Whatever do you want to say to Sir Robert de Baudicourt?'

'I need a safe conduct from him so that I can leave the province.'

'Leave the province? Child, what madcap scheme have you in your head?'

'A plan, cousin, not a wild scheme. You must have heard the tradition about the virgin who will come out of Lorraine to save France.'

'I reckon everybody has heard that tale,' Durand said, puzzled.

Joan took a deep breath, walked over to the small window opening into the narrow street. 'Cousin, I am that virgin,' she said simply. 'I have been chosen by God to lead the French armies to victory, and see the Dauphin crowned at Rheims.'

She stopped, waiting for some exclamation of surprise or disbelief, but Durand merely rubbed his chin thoughtfully and stared at her.

'If I make my way to the Governor he will give me a horse and an escort so that I may travel in safety,' Joan said, eagerly.

'You'll need protection along the roads,' he agreed.

'You don't seem surprised,' she said, puzzled. 'You do believe me, don't you?'

Durand scratched his head as if uncertain how to reply, then began to speak, groping for words.

'I never was a handsome man, Joan, nor one who could make pretty speeches. Most girls used to laugh at me when I tried to court them, until I reckoned I'd have to make do with a widow or an ugly wench. Then I met your cousin.'

'Yes?'

'Jehan was the loveliest thing I'd ever seen. Always laughing, and walking as if she were about to begin to dance. I never thought she'd look at me twice. I told myself she was too young for me and too giddy, but I couldn't stop the feeling for her growing inside me. And I never knew, never even guessed, that she felt the same way until your Aunt Aveline asked me if I would like to marry her daughter. I never believed she was really mine, all mine, until we'd been wed a twelvemonth and I saw her looking at me one day. Not saying anything but looking at me, calm and loving, and—and clean like water. I believed then that she really loved me. I saw it in her face. And you have the same look in your eyes now. And I believe you.'

'And you'll help me?'

'It won't be easy. Sir Robert is an important man. We can't simply march up to the garrison and demand to see him.'

'But I *have* to see him! I have to tell him who I am so that he can give me a horse, and an escort—'

'I know, I know. Let me think for a minute.'

Durand sat down and furrowed his brows while Joan tapped her fingers impatiently on the sill.

'I've got it!' he said, at last. 'There's a lieutenant at the garrison, close personal friend of Sir Robert. He owes me a favour. I got him some foodstuffs cheaply a few weeks ago, and he was very grateful, having overspent his portion.'

'What's his name? Can we go and see him at once?'

'Better let me talk to him. Bertrand de Poulengy doesn't

know you as I do, and he's liable to be a mite disbelieving until I've talked to him. In fact, there's no need to say very much at all. I'll just tell him that my young cousin is anxious to meet the Governor.'

'Then go now,' Joan urged. 'Go and find this de Poulengy and make him take me to the Governor. Go now!'

By the time she laid down to sleep that night, Joan had been assured by a perspiring Durand, who had found his errand a difficult one, that Sir Robert would see her the following morning.

She was tingling with excitement as they climbed the hill to the square-topped garrison where there was a constant bustle of activity as more soldiers than Joan had ever seen hurried up and down. Some of them glanced at Joan curiously and her cheeks burned when she heard a ribald remark tossed casually in her direction.

At the main gate a pleasant-featured man stepped forward to greet them.

'Bertrand de Poulengy, at your service, Ma'am'selle. Your cousin tells me you wish to see Sir Robert. You'll understand the Governor is a very busy man and has to limit his time carefully.'

'I also have very little time,' Joan said, simply.

De Poulengy looked at her with fresh interest. She had not, at first glance attracted his attention, being a big, raw-boned peasant girl with no claim to beauty, but her voice was pleasing and she moved proudly. He wondered if de Baudicourt would find her to his taste.

The Governor was seated behind a flat-topped desk in his office over the garderobe when de Poulengy ushered Joan and Durand in.

Joan glanced briefly around the room, noting with approval the lack of ornament in the furnishings and the newly burnished chain-mail on its stand. Then she came eagerly to the desk. leaning her palms on its smooth top and studying the man behind it intently.

'You are the young lady who is here on a visit from Domremy?'

'I am Joan, the virgin from Lorraine.'

'Has Lorraine only one virgin then? I hadn't dreamed its women were so accommodating!'

Sir Robert laughed loudly at his own witticism and winked at de Poulengy. Joan drew back a little, surprised at his obtuseness.

'I am *the* virgin from Lorraine. I have a request to make.'

'If it's a question of interfering between your parents and yourself over some man you wish to marry, I must warn you—'

'You don't understand,' Joan cried, fiercely, 'I don't want a suitor.'

'Then what do you want?'

'I need about a dozen soldiers,' she began.

'A dozen! Do you seriously expect me to accept you as a virgin when your needs are so exorbitant?'

'And I need a horse, and a safe conduct,' she rushed on, 'so that I may go to Chinon to see the Dauphin.'

'And what do you expect to get from the Dauphin?'

'A better horse,' Joan said promptly, 'and an army of men.'

'Now why should the Dauphin do that?' Sir Robert asked, patiently.

'Because God has sent me to drive the goddams out of France and to see the Dauphin crowned at Rheims.'

She threw back her head proudly and waited. Sir Robert stared at her for a second or two, and then started to laugh, slapping his knee and spluttering.

'God told me that I was the virgin out of Lorraine who would save the throne of France,' Joan said, again.

But her voice could scarcely be heard above Sir Robert's mirth. The other two looked embarrassed and uneasy, and Durand had begun to twist his cap round and round in his hands.

'You must let me go to the Dauphin! You must give me a horse and some men!' Joan persisted, but her voice trembled on the edge of tears.

Sir Robert's jocularity exploded into anger. He sprang up, pushing his chair backwards so violently that it tipped over.

'Must? Must? Who are you to tell me what I must or must not do? Have I not enough worry with Jean de Verger of Burgundy threatening my borders? Have I not enough trouble trying to raise more troops to defend this province? Must I also be bothered by crazy young women? You should have realized, Bertrand, that the girl was a crank! You, Lassois, whatever your name is, take your cousin home and give her a good smacking to bring her to her senses!'

De Poulengy was already edging them towards the door. Joan made one last attempt.

'If I could speak privately to you, sir?'

Sir Robert's face purpled.

'Set one foot within this garrison again and I'll hand you over to my archers for their sport!'

The door had banged behind them. The opportunity had passed and would never come back. She had wasted the precious interview, and there would never be another one. Sir Robert would never agree to seeing her again.

She had been so sure that the Governor would believe her and grant her requests, that she had not bothered to rehearse in her mind the words she intended to use. She had imagined that she would need no eloquence but would merely state her mission. Her cousin, who was a slow, simple man, had recognized at once that she spoke the truth. Yet Sir Robert de Baudicourt, who was well-educated and important, had lost his temper and shouted at her.

'I'm sorry, my dear,' de Poulengy was saying, 'but Sir Robert is a quick-tempered man and has much on his mind.' He was sorry for the girl who looked dispirited and was surreptitiously wiping tears from her lashes with the corner of her shawl. 'If you had given me some inkling of what your cousin intended to say,' he said crossly to Durand, 'I would have told you that you were wasting your time.'

Durand began to apologize noisily, but Joan remained silent.

She had never been so miserable in her whole life. She had been so certain that when she left Vaucouleurs she would ride out with an escort of soldiers, bound for Chinon, as her voices had promised.

I was not worthy for the task, Joan thought sorrowfully. God sent His archangels and His saints and I was not worthy. My first fears were right, for I am not fit to lead armies or talk with princes.

'What will you do now, cousin?' Durand asked, as they took leave of de Poulengy and walked down the hill towards Burey-le-Petit.

'Go home at the end of the week when my father comes for me,' she said, disconsolately, and her shoulders drooped so miserably that he hadn't the heart to question her further, but began to point out various landmarks as they passed through the town.

Joan felt herself to be a dismal guest during the remainder of her visit although Jehan didn't seem to notice and Durand said nothing.

Yet it was almost a relief when she saw the wagon pull up before her cousin's small house. Her eyes widened with pleasure as she recognized the figure driving the horse, and she ran out eagerly to greet him.

'Michel! What in the world are you doing at Vaucouleurs?'

'Your father gave me permission to call for you. You're not angry?'

'Oh, no! I'm so pleased that you came.'

'That sounds as if you missed me!' He jumped down and hugged her, noting that she didn't push him away as she was in the habit of doing.

59

'I didn't think about you, but now that I see you—oh, come inside, and have some wine! You met my cousin before, didn't you? Jehan, this is Michel Lebuin, a neighbour of ours.'

And a prospective suitor, Jehan thought, being, like most happily married girls extremely interested in the matrimonial prospects of her relatives. She liked the frank smiling face of the young man and the way his eyes followed Joan as she bustled about the room.

Joan was chattering in a gay, excited fashion. She had been rather quiet during the visit and Jehan believed she had guessed the reason. Obviously, Joan had been missing the company of her friends.

As the two of them drove away, Jehan squeezed her husband's arm gleefully. 'Do you think they will have the wedding before the harvest is in?'

Joan's gaiety had evaporated. She sat, hunched and silent, beside Michel, trying not to look in the direction of the garrison. But it was no use, for her eyes continually turned towards the high grey walls behind which the Governor lived.

Perhaps she should have made a further attempt to see Sir Robert. Perhaps she should have returned to the garrison, battering her fists against the doors, shouting her message until everybody believed her.

If only her voices would speak to her now, or if her legs would experience that strange compulsion to move in an unknown direction! But her legs felt heavy as lead, and there was no sound but the gentle clip-clop of the horse and Michel's tuneless whistling.

It's over, she told herself firmly. I was foolish to imagine that I could ever perform such a task. It's over! Now I must go home and look after the sheep again and stop thinking that I'm different from other girls.

With a great sadness and a rising relief, she turned towards Michel.

'Are they all right at home? I was so pleased to see you

that I forgot to ask.'

'Your father is in a fine temper because the door of the new barn blew off in the gale last night. Your mother told me to tell you, by the way, that Jacabina has had her puppies. Your brother, Pierre, has kept the smallest of the litter for you. He said it was the one you would want to keep.'

'Pierre knows me well! And you, Michel, are you all right? Did you go to the fair?'

'I thought over what you'd said. I mean, about saving my money, so I stayed at home.'

'But I was only joking,' she protested.

'I wasn't,' Michel said, quietly.

The horse had slowed to a walk and the reins hung slackly between his fingers.

'I intend to save my money, Joan,' he rushed on. 'I want to use it to buy some pretty things for the cottage.'

'What cottage?'

'I told you that my father has promised me some land, those two big meadows down by the west stream. It's good soil and well-drained, and I've already marked out a site for a cottage. We could begin to build it at once, and watch the walls growing up during the summer.'

'They say there is fresh danger from the Burgundians,' she evaded. 'Is it wise to want to build houses when we may be overrun by enemies? When I was in Vaucouleurs, I heard some rumours.'

'There has been war as long as we can remember! As long as our parents can remember!' Michel said, impatiently. 'We can't go single to our graves because we're afraid of the future. I want you to be my wife, Joan. I've never looked at another girl. You told me you'd give me an answer. Please, Joan!'

She had never been closer to loving him before, nor had he ever spoken at such length or with such vigour.

'What would you do,' she asked abruptly, 'if I told you I had had dreams of—of being something more than a labourer's wife? Of being something other than myself? Of going where I never expected to go, and doing what no woman has ever done before?'

'Most girls have fancies,' he said, comfortably. 'Boys, too! I used to imagine riding off as a troubadour or something but I always knew I'd settle down as a farmer like my father and my brothers. You won't have time for such dreams when you have children about your skirts. Come, Joan, give me an answer.'

She took a deep breath and said, trying to sound calm and confident, 'Tell your father that you'd like him to give you that land at once.'

Even as he flung his arm about her shoulders, she heard the voices sobbing inside her head.

CHAPTER FOUR

NEUFCHATEAU, JULY, 1428

THE inn was crowded to the doors, and in between greeting and serving her customers, Madame La Rousse found time to make a rough calculation of her profits. It was, she decided tritely, an ill-wind that blew nobody any good. If the Burgundians had not attacked Vaucouleurs, the village of Domremy would not have been evacuated and she would not now have a dwelling crammed to the roof with refugees.

She inserted her ample bulk skilfully between the tables, pausing occasionally to refill a wine jug or listen to a snatch of gossip. It was hard to remember, amid the convivial chatter, that the Burgundians were scarcely ten miles distant. If they reached Domremy, they might easily sweep on through Greux to Neufchateau, and then there would be no more profits because Madame La Rousse would prefer to tear down the inn with her bare hands rather than serve Burgundians in it.

Meanwhile, one might as well take advantage of the situation and encourage everybody to drink their fill. She noted with approval that the girl she had engaged as temporary help was also urging people to drink up.

With all the extra work, Madame had been pleased when one of the refugees had offered her services as barmaid. A hefty girl and a quick, cheerful worker, even if she was no beauty, thought the proprietor, and respectable too. She had already rebuked one of the regulars for using bad language, and dealt firmly but tactfully with two men arguing over their respective villages by reminding them they were all Frenchmen.

'Go through to the back and get yourself a bite of supper, Joan,' Madame said, now, and was confirmed in her good opinion when the girl smiled but finished serving her customers before she obeyed.

In the small kitchen, Joan poured herself some ale and cut herself a couple of slices of bread. There was cheese and small red onions in a side trencher, and she drenched them liberally with vinegar, then carried her supper out to the back porch where she leaned gratefully against the step and munched hungrily.

In the yard, a variety of ducks, hens and chickens pattered about and from the byre came the sleepy cries of horses, sheep and cows, herded in higgledy-piggledy. There would be a fine to-do when it was time to sort them out and take them home.

Then the yard and the byre faded from her consciousness, and she saw her familiars again. They floated before her, small enough to hold in her hands, each one a perfect replica of the tall, proud figures she had embraced at Bermont. Their faces were sad and tears like sparkling pinpoints fell down their cheeks, drenching the gold.

When they appeared in this guise, she felt an almost maternal tenderness for them, and her heart was heavy with guilt. 'I am not worthy,' she said over and over.

'Who are you to judge your own qualities and seek to change what must be?' their voices answered her. 'Humility lies in acceptance, not in denial!'

The figures were fading, passing between her fingers like smoke.

'I need a sign,' she said, desperately. 'I am not strong enough to begin my task again until some sign is given to me.'

'Why on earth are you talking to yourself?' Hauviette cried merrily, coming up behind Joan and regarding her with affectionate curiosity.

'I didn't hear you!'

As always, when she was wrenched back to the everyday world, she felt bewildered and forlorn.

'There's a friend of yours here, asking for you. A soldier,

64

and quite a handsome one! You're a sly one to say nothing about him! Did you meet him when you went to Vaucouleurs?'

'Where is this man? Did he give you his name?'

'Bertrand de Poulengy he said.' Hauviette blinked as Joan sprang up and brushed past her with a glowing face. 'I never saw you rush to meet Michel so eagerly!' she cried teasingly, but her friend had gone.

De Poulengy was seated at a small table in an alcove and rose politely as Joan slipped into the seat opposite him. From the bar counter Madame La Rousse watched them curiously. She hoped she had not been mistaken in her estimation of the d'Arc girl's character, but the man looked decent enough.

'You wished to see me?' Joan said, for the look on the soldier's face gave her the odd impression that he had forgotten why he was there.

'We learned the people of Domremy had fled to Neufchateau, and the little maid I questioned told me you were staying here.'

'That was Hauviette. She's my best friend.'

'I am on my way back to Vaucouleurs to rejoin Sir Robert and have not much time to waste,' he said gravely. 'The situation is very bad, worse than most people realize. Since the Anglo-Burgundian alliance, the Dauphinists have been squeezed helplessly between the might of the goddams and the treachery of the Burgundians.'

'I know that, but you didn't ride out of your way to give me the latest war-gossip. Why did you come?'

De Poulengy spread his hands wide and looked even more bewildered.

'I wish I could answer you in a few simple words. But I can't, because I'm not sure why I came. I only know that I told a friend of mine about your visit to the Governor. I told it as a joke, you understand, meaning to make him laugh. But it didn't sound like a joke and we didn't laugh. And when I had finished speaking, I knew that I had said something important. Jean de Metz, that is the name of my friend, wishes to meet you if ever you come to Vaucouleurs again.'

'My parents would not allow it,' she said. 'And there is talk of my marriage. I must marry if I am not to be pushed into a nunnery or laughed at as an old maid.'

'Then I was wrong. I thought I saw something in you that isn't there at all.'

'What did you see?' she asked, curiously.

'I don't know,' he said. 'It was strong and clean and full of hope, but I can't express it in words. I don't know what it was, and I don't know why I came.'

'You were sent,' Joan said quietly.

'Not at all! It was my own idea entirely!' he began indignantly, but she shook her head, smiling.

'God is very good,' she said, at last, 'for He gives people faith in me so that I may have faith in myself.'

'And you will return to Vaucouleurs and meet Jean de Metz?'

'When I am ready, I'll return.'

'And you won't wait too long?'

She shook her head again, and he touched her hand briefly and hurried out.

'Your young man is here,' Madame La Rousse said.

'Young man?'

'Perhaps I should have said "other young man",' Madame added roguishly. 'Quite a popular young lady, aren't you?'

'Oh, you mean Michel Lebuin. He said he might look in.'

'Well, aren't you going to meet him?'

'I'll help you with the washing-up first.'

'Nonsense, girl! You've been on your feet all day. Anyway, from the look of things, these are liable to sit here all night. In times of emergency, there's more liquor drunk and more babies fathered than you'd credit! Now go along and say goodnight to your friends, and then you'd best be off to bed.'

She gave Joan a good-natured pat on the shoulder, and

hurried back to her customers.

Michel was scuffing his feet in the lane and looked up sulkily as she came out.

'It's almost dark, Joan. Surely that old harridan in there isn't going to make you slave all night!'

'Madame La Rousse is going to pay me for my help, so she has a right to expect me to work,' Joan said, mildly.

'I don't like the idea of you working in an inn,' he said, in a discontented tone. 'I've seen the way some of the customers look at these bar-girls. I don't like to think of them looking at you in that fashion.'

'Oh, Michel, not now! I'm tired!'

'Not too tired to chat with the men and make jokes,' he persisted.

She sighed, letting his voice run on and on, while she wondered miserably if all men acted in so jealous and suspicious a fashion towards the women they hoped to marry.

If only she had been born a boy! Boys had so much more freedom than girls. They were taught to ride and to handle weapons, and if they went off to fight people applauded them.

'What would you say,' she asked abruptly, 'if I told you that I was destined to restore the crown of France to the Dauphin?'

'I'd say you shouldn't sample that wine you've been serving!'

'Michel, when you look at me, do you ever see anything in my face?' she questioned.

'What am I supposed to see?'

'I don't know. A look, a thought, a dream. I don't know.'

'I don't understand you,' he said again, and his face was resentful. 'I don't know what you want any longer. You've changed, Joan.'

'No. I've merely become more myself,' she said, quietly.

'I know you speak in riddles, and look at me as if I wasn't there, and sneak off by yourself into the fields. We used to be so happy, Joan, and now it's all spoiled. Is it another man? Have you met somebody you love better than me?'

'Oh, Michel, dear Michel!' she cried. 'There is no other man. There is nobody in the world I ever considered as a husband except you.'

'But you don't love me.'

'I'm sorry, Michel. I'm so sorry!'

She began to cry, hating herself for causing him pain.

'My father gave me the land when he might have sold it for a profit. The foundations of the cottage are laid. My mother is going to give us the cradle in which I was rocked for our first child. Everybody expects—'

'Everybody expects! Nobody asks me what I expect! Nobody asks me what I want! They push me, and worry me, and hammer at me! They make me into a mould and call it Joan and never give me time to shape myself! There is no man! There is no man! There is nobody, and I can't get it into your head.'

She stopped abruptly, her eyes fixed on the sky. The darkening heavens glowed with a fierce red light that grew brighter even as she stared.

People were hurrying out of the inn, pointing down the hill and babbling in excitement.

'It's Domremy,' Michel said, and his voice sounded old and tired. 'There's a fire down in the village.'

'There will be no village by morning,' sobbed a woman.

'The Burgundians have fired our homes!' cried a dozen voices. 'There will be no Domremy! There will be no church where we can worship! There will be nothing left of anything that once was ours!

'Is there nobody who can save us from our enemies?' a youth cried hysterically.

The cry was taken up, as the citizens surged back and forth in the narrow street.

'Who will save us and bring an end to all this misery?'

Against the sky, the flames burned more brightly.

'But you cannot sit here and let the English take away your lands one by one, until there is nothing left of your Kingdom except a castle and a couple of meadows!'

'Agnes, dear Agnes! You are a delightful creature, but when you preach politics, you look uncommonly like my mother-in-law!'

'You're very fond of your mother-in-law!'

'Lady Yolande is more tender to me than my own mother ever was. But I don't take her to bed with me.'

'Meaning that I, being your leman, am not allowed to have a mind and an opinion of my own?'

Indignantly, Agnes Sorel pushed away the Dauphin's arm and paced the apartment, her wooden heels tapping angrily and her long skirts crackling.

Truly a magnificent creature! Charles watched her with pleasure, admiring her white shoulders and the masses of red hair swirling down her back.

'If I had enough money,' he mused, 'I would buy you emeralds. Ropes of emeralds! To twine in your hair and encircle your neck until you glowed in green fire.'

'Dreams, Charles. When did a man ever buy emeralds with dreams? You have no money to pay your servants. Your armies have melted away, and your Kingdom becomes smaller so rapidly that soon you'll be able to stroll round it in a day!'

Charles rolled lazily on to his back and grinned.

'Now you sound like my wife,' he observed. 'Poor Marie never knows when to stop nagging.'

'The Dauphine has cause to nag,' Agnes snapped. 'What kind of a King allows his enemies to run circles about him while he lolls on cushions and eats sweets?'

Guiltily, Charles moved the piece of marzipan from one side of his mouth to the other.

'I might try another treaty,' he suggested.

'Now that the English hold Paris and Campiegne, and encircle Orleans, what sort of a treaty do you think they will accept? Oh, Charles, why can't you be a real monarch? Dismiss La Tremouille, for he is hand-in-glove with the Burgundians. And send de Chartres away, for he thinks more of his fine robes than his duties as a man of God.'

'Ah, yes! I remember that the Archbishop preached a sermon against you last Sunday. What was it he called you?'

'A piece of slime spawned up from the gutter,' Agnes said, resentfully. 'And he is a fine one to talk. Everybody knows what he uses the back door of his episcopal palace to bring in and out!'

She came back to the Dauphin and leaned her head against his knees.

'I am not ashamed of being what I am,' she said, at last. 'I could have left you many times, but I stayed with you because I love you. I wish I could respect you as well.'

'You're nagging me again,' he said, petulantly. 'Come and lie down and soothe me with your sweet compliments. I have many to tell me what I should or should not do. That is what they're paid for—when I have the money! I keep you for a different purpose.'

'You're hopeless!' Pouting, she climbed up beside him and nibbled his ear.

'I can't afford emeralds,' he murmured, 'but I think I can run to a rope of garnets. Would you like garnets, my love?'

'Sire, forgive me for disturbing you, but Count Dunois is here.'

The Dauphine Marie stood politely in the doorway.

'Jean here? I thought he was at Orleans. He is Governor of the town.'

'He has a new plan for breaking the English blockade,' Marie said, earnestly.

'No doubt!' Charles relinquished his mistress with a sigh

and met his wife's gentle blue eyes. 'My cousin makes excellent plans, but as they can't succeed unless we double the size of the army, I fail to see what use they are.'

'Gilles de Raiz is with him. They've brought maps.'

'I'm sick of looking at maps,' the Dauphin yawned. 'All those wavy lines and places one has never heard about and would never wish to visit!'

'I gave orders for a meal to be prepared for them,' Marie said. 'I hope you approve.'

'Oh, *I* approve! But it is the cook you will have to woo. I owe him some money.'

'You're keeping everybody waiting,' Agnes cried. 'Do tidy yourself, darling, and try to pretend you're a real monarch!'

The two women, between them, managed to get Charles into a reasonably neat and respectable state, and pushed him, still reluctant, through the door.

'Will you be joining them, Madame?'

'I don't like Gilles de Raiz,' the Dauphine said, with a little shudder. 'Dunois is always very kind and friendly, but there is something in de Raiz that chills me.'

'I feel it too,' Agnes agreed.

'If only they can persuade my husband to do something positive!' the Dauphine cried. 'Sometimes I wish that women could give orders and ride to war. As it is, we can only try to influence the men we love.'

'And they do not listen to us!' Agnes said, bitterly.

The two young women sat down on the tumbled bed and clasped hands in sympathy.

NANCY, JANUARY, 1429

Jacques Alain had always prided himself on being a stolid practical and unemotional man. He had never been a man who questioned the nature of things or attempted to analyse his feelings. He had married a girl from the same village, maintained a farm there, and brought up a large family of children almost unthinkingly, for he never stopped to ask himself if he loved his wife or was proud of his land. It was sufficient for him that they existed.

When the English soldiers had burned down the village, he had moved on with his wife and children and the orphan lad they had taken in six years before. What a mercy, thought Alain, that the boy Simon had run away while they were still refugees. He had slipped away in the night and they had never seen him since. There might have been trouble had he stayed for Alain's daughters were growing into comely young women and he had already found husbands of substance for two of them.

Alain was well on the way to becoming a man of substance again himself. He had settled at Vaucouleurs and at first it had been hard, taking any job he could find while his women-folk used their skill at lace mending, until he had saved enough money to buy a little property of his own. He had concentrated upon the rebuilding of his prosperity and was looked upon now as a leading citizen. Even Sir Robert de Baudicourt passed the time of day as he rode past. Two of the Alain boys rode with the de Baudicourt troop and both had received slight wounds in the fighting with the Burgundians. Madame Alain had two silk dresses and a parlour at the back of the house where she could sit gossiping with her friends, Jehan Lassois and Catherine le Royer.

Which made it all the more peculiar that he, Jacques Alain, should now be escorting a completely unknown and decidedly insane young woman to Nancy! To begin with, Nancy was an Anglo-Burgundian stronghold and Alain had very little faith in the ability of the Burgundians to recognize a safe conduct when they saw one. Then it was a cold, damp season that insinuated itself into his bones, making them creak and ache. Then, the roof of the barn had been leaking for some time and he had promised himself he would attend to it before the spring floods.

Yet, here he was, jogging along through the fine rain with Durand Lassois on one side and himself on the other of a young girl whose appearance startled Alain to the depths of his conventional soul every time he looked at her. If one of his own daughters had ever—but no! Marguerite, Susanna and Yvette would as soon have thought of cutting off their pretty heads as cutting off their hair. This girl had cropped hers as high as the ears and pulled a black cap down over it. And she was clad, most shockingly, in a black tunic and dark grey hose that exposed her long legs to the thighs. She had well-shaped legs, Alain thought, and wondered why they roused no desire in him. Ah well! perhaps he was growing older.

He tried to remember just when he had stopped being the onlooker who listened to the tales of his neighbour, Lassois, and become instead a participant in what was clearly a mad adventure.

First there had been his wife, chatting as they sat together after the shutters had been drawn.

'Catherine le Royer told me today that she is expecting a visitor. A cousin to Jehan Lassois is coming to Vaucouleurs for a long visit. She had planned to help Jehan when the child is born, but as a midwife has been engaged already an unmarried girl would be rather in the way. So the le Royers offered to put her up. Apparently the cousin came to stay for a week last spring. It must have been when you were laid up with that bad shoulder, for I can't remember meeting her.'

Then had come Catherine le Royer, plumply flustered, asking for the loan of Madame Alain's best goblets.

'For my own are certainly not grand enough to set out before Sir Robert de Baudicourt! I almost fainted away with the shock of it when I heard the Governor himself intended to visit our little home. Jean de Metz—that handsome young captain from the garrison—told my husband that the Governor wishes to meet Joan.'

'The girl who is staying with you?'

73

'That one. And I may tell you that since she arrived my house has been turned upside down. First it was Captain de Poulengy rushing in to greet her as if she were his long lost sister, and then Captain de Metz arriving and sending me out of the room, if you please, while he talked privately to her.'

'Where is she from, this girl?'

'From Domremy, the village that was fired by the Burgundians last year. Her father, Jacques d'Arc, is quite a respected citizen there, so what he can be thinking of to let his daughter go traipsing about unchaperoned, I can't imagine.'

'Is she pretty?' Madame Alain had asked.

'Lord bless you, no! Her nose is too big and her neck is too short, but she has lovely eyes. One has to admit that! And she's quiet too, with pleasant manners. Yet she seems to attract noise and bustle around her like a honeypot attracts bees. I do wish I knew why Sir Robert wishes to see her, but no doubt I'll be sent out of the room again!'

Then had come Durand Lassois, who looked his usual slightly stupid self but had astonishing information to impart.

'My cousin, Joan, intends to ride to Chinon where the Dauphin will allow her to accompany the army that the English may be driven out. She has first to obtain a safe conduct out of the province from Sir Robert, but as soon as he makes up his mind, de Metz and de Poulengy will go with her.'

Alain had found it almost impossible to believe that Lassois, who wouldn't even bet on a race lest he lose his money, should be seriously considering allowing his young relative to embark on such a scheme.

'My cousin sought out the Governor when she came last year, but Sir Robert was not ready to listen to her then.'

'And he will listen now?'

'He has seen her several times and talked to her, and his mind begins to waver.'

Alain felt his own mind shake a little when his neighbour then asked him, as if it had been the most natural request in the world, to lend one of his horses to the girl.

'Apparently the Duke of Lorraine wishes to meet Joan, and Sir Robert will allow her to ride to Nancy.'

'Then why doesn't Sir Robert give her the use of one of his own mounts?'

'He is unwilling to risk the loss of a valuable beast,' Lassois said, with sublime lack of tact.

Alain had meant to resent the implied slur on his own livestock; he had meant to refuse the request. But he found himself offering to act as escort. He heard himself make the offer as if he were listening to somebody else, and when Lassois had accepted and gone away, he had sat down and wondered seriously if he was sickening for something.

He meant to withdraw the offer and carry on quietly with his work, but events seemed to take hold of him, sweeping him along.

The girl Joan arrived, shook his hand in a business-like fashion, calmly appropriated his own horse, leaving him the docile mare he had chosen as most suitable for a female, and taken complete charge of events in a way that left him gasping.

She turned slightly in the saddle now, scratching her leg vigorously.

'There are more fleas on this suit than hairs on my head,' she complained, merrily. 'I took it from Jean de Metz's squire, and I'll swear it's not been brushed since it was made.'

'It would have been more seemly to wear a skirt,' Alain said disapprovingly.

'Nonsense! How far do you imagine we would have travelled if I had been hampered by woman's clothing?' she retorted. 'My life will soon be passed among men, as a man, so the sooner I get used to breeches the better!'

'The Duke of Lorraine may not allow us to leave his territory,' Alain said, unconsciously casting about in his mind for something else to grumble about.

'The Duke is curious about me,' Joan said with satisfaction. 'His spies must have heard of me, and like a sensible man he wishes to see me for himself.'

'Perhaps you can persuade him to change sides,' Alain suggested.

Ignoring the sarcasm, she laughed again.

'The good Duke is past sixty and in bad health, but his son-in-law might be persuaded. Rene d'Anjou is a fine warrior they say, and he is brother to the Dauphine Marie. Sir Robert told me that d'Anjou was reared by the Duke of Lorraine, but now that he is older, he has shown some sympathy for our cause.'

'You have great faith in your powers of persuasion.'

'I have great faith!' she answered shortly, and her lips narrowed into a thin line.

They rode on through the rain, and Alain felt a little shiver of apprehension as the gates of Nancy loomed up ahead.

'Don't be afraid!' Joan said, although he hadn't realized she was looking at him.

'I don't like Burgundians,' Alain muttered.

'Neither do I, but that's no reason to be frightened of them,' Joan said, serenely. 'We'll come to no harm at Nancy. We'll find lodgings for the night, then you'll both take me to the Duke.'

'It'll be late, cousin,' Durand protested.

'If the Duke has sent for me, then he can stay out of bed long enough to welcome me,' she said shortly.

Fortunately, they discovered lodgings fairly quickly, and were then directed to the castle by an inquisitive ostler longing to know their business.

Alain had not intended to ride to Nancy, but he thought it rather hard that, having endured an uncomfortable journey, he should not even catch a glimpse of the Duke. He was annoyed when, upon reaching the postern gate,

Joan was promptly admitted while he and Durand were left kicking their heels outside.

The guards seemed to know something of their errand, for several loud remarks concerning holy virgins were bandied about. Durand tugged his companion's arm nervously, and they moved aimlessly away and leaned against an inconspicuous wall.

The remaining light flickered and died, and the guards were no more than bulky silhouettes. It was still raining and the wind blew chill and menacing.

'She's a long time,' Alain said, at last.

'Reckon they've a lot to discuss,' Durand said, comfortably.

'It might be a trap. They might not let her go.'

'They've no reason to keep her,' Durand said.

They fell silent again, in the manner of countrymen, while stars blazed over the turrets. Then Alain started to talk, aided by an occasional grunt from his companion.

'I didn't mean to lend your cousin a horse. I didn't mean to ride into a Burgundian town. But here I am, standing outside a Duke's palace and not knowing why I agreed to all this! And I agreed even before I met your cousin. My tongue ran away with me, and my feet have run away with me, and nothing makes any sense. But I keep thinking, my friend, that if Joan can cause me to act in such a way, there might be a chance that others will follow her. There might even be a chance that the Dauphin will win his Kingdom. Do you think there might be such an outcome?'

They stiffened suddenly as the gate across the yard was opened, and a figure on a horse cantered out. Another horse was being led out behind her by a groom.

'Joan? Is everything well?'

'Shall we seek our lodgings now?' Durand asked, in the hopeful tone of a man who has not dared, until this moment, to admit to himself that he is tired.

'We ride back to Vaucouleurs!' Joan said, shortly.

'But the horses will not stand the pace,' Alain exclaimed.

'Then we leave at first light,' she said, abruptly. 'You had better take your own horse back. As you see, the Duke has given me another one.'

Not another word would she say until they were back in the lodging house. Alain came in from the stables where he had been supervising the horses, to find Durand placidly eating a substantial meal while Joan raged up and down, throwing out sentences between mouthfuls of bread.

'A horse! The Duke patted me on the head as if I were a good little girl and gave me a horse! Oh, and four francs! You had better keep them, cousin! And do you know why the fine Duke wanted to see me? He had heard there was a witch girl at Vaucouleurs who might cure him of his sickness? And do you know what he suffers from? He has the English disease! He told me about it and begged me to cure him! To remove the results of his own personal filth!'

'And did you cure him, Joan?'

'I told him to go back to his lawful wife and give up his mistress. He said he loved the woman. Loved her, and him past sixty! I told him he ought to be ashamed of himself. How can he expect to be cured if he still clings to the cause of his disease! And I told him that I had no time to waste on petty matters!'

'You used such words to a royal duke!'

Alain groped for the wine jug.

'A Burgundian duke!' Joan said, with lofty scorn. 'He's just a sick, old man, afraid for his body and not caring enough for his soul. I told him I wanted him to send me his son-in-law, d'Anjou. The young man is not here at the moment, and I regret it for I would have been able to talk good sense to him. But the old duke waggled his head and his finger at me, and told me that d'Anjou will make up his own mind.'

'And what did you say?'

'I told him that I hoped d'Anjou would show better sense and a more unselfish attitude than his father-in-law!'

Joan said, biting ferociously into her crust.

'Perhaps we ought to leave at once,' Durand said. 'The Duke may not allow us out of the town, once he has had leisure to think over what you've said to him.'

'Half an hour ago, you said the horses needed rest!' Joan exclaimed. 'Now you want to run away, because you're afraid of a little plain speaking! Well, we must give credit where it's due. The duke is a fool, but he heard me out, and I promised to pray to God for him if he really made an effort to improve his conduct.'

Alain began to feel a lively sympathy for the hapless duke. But Joan was already tracing with her finger on the table a short cut she had noticed on the way that would take them back to Vaucouleurs more speedily.

The next morning, feeling as if he had not closed his eyes for more than half an hour, Alain came out into the stable-yard where Joan was already mounted on her new black horse. A groom, holding the bridle of his horse, loosed the rein and ducked back within the doorway of the shed.

'Hurry up, friend,' Joan called. 'We have been awake for hours, Durand and I.'

Glancing at his neighbour's drawn face and half-suppressed yawn, Alain rather doubted the latter part of her sentence.

'I could not have slept anyway,' Joan was grumbling, 'for I have done nothing but scratch all night. You will have to buy me some new clothes when we reach Vaucouleurs.'

Alain opened his mouth, then shut it again in resignation. It was useless trying to argue. If Joan had decided he was going to buy her a new suit, then sooner or later that was exactly what he would do.

As they rode out of the inn yard, the groom emerged from the stable and wiped his hand across his face.

Simon had recognized his old protector at once, and for a brief instant had longed to rush forward, claiming recognition. Then he had slunk hastily aside, for how could he explain his presence in an Anglo-Burgundian town to the man who had once seen his home destroyed by the goddams? How could he explain that he had never reached Vaucouleurs, but had been seized by a Burgundian raiding party and carried back across the border? And in the years that followed, he had worked for the Burgundians, never starving, but never prospering, never feeling any loyalty to any cause, nor needing affection. And by the time the three riders were out of sight, he had quite forgotten his arrested impulse to run forward and reveal himself to Jacques Alain.

CHAPTER FIVE

CHINON, MARCH, 1429

'B u t, my darling, if you intend to see this girl, you can't sprawl about on your bed for the rest of the day!'

Agnes Sorel put her hands on her hips and shook her head in exasperation.

The Dauphin spat a grape pip elegantly into the fruit-bowl, and sat up.

'I haven't made up my mind if I want to see her,' he said.

'Lord help us! We went all through that yesterday,' Agnes exclaimed. 'You decided that, as she had travelled so far, you would give her an audience.'

'*You* decided that,' Charles said irritably. 'You and Marie, between you, have bothered and pestered me for a week. Why I have to waste my time with a crazy woman—'

'Sir Robert de Baudicourt doesn't think she's crazy,' Agnes interrupted. 'He said in his letter that the girl Joan had made a great impression upon him.'

'Sir Robert has spent so long at Vaucouleurs that his brains are addled.'

'And de Metz and de Poulengy have escorted her here and even paid the expenses of the journey out of their own pockets.'

'Which proves that their brains are addled too!'

'And in her message the girl said she would recognize you among all others, even though she has never seen you.'

'Which is why, at this very moment, my steward is trying on my robes and looking forward to the one great moment of his life when he sits on the throne.'

'While you skulk at the back? Oh, Charles, why must you put her to the test? Why does everything have to be proved twice over for you before you can believe it? Isn't it enough that she already struck a man dead?'

'Rubbish!'

'But it's not rubbish, Charles! As the girl rode into the town, one of the guards shouted that if that was the virgin from Lorraine, she was welcome to join him and lose her maidenhead, God be damned if she wasn't! And the girl shouted back that he ought not to blaspheme when he was so near to his death. And within the hour—'

'And within the hour the man fell off his horse into the moat and drowned! I heard it from d'Alençon. It might have been a more convincing miracle if the fellow hadn't spent the intervening hour being treated to rounds of drinks by all the friends who wanted to hear how he'd ticked off the crazy girl!'

'But he did *die*! What more do you need?'

'A great deal more than you and Marie seem to expect. I wish you'd leave me to make up my own mind about my own affairs.'

'Then *make* up your mind. Either see her or send her away. But don't just sit around, making everybody anxious and impatient. This Joan might really be a messenger from God.'

'That's not very likely,' Charles observed. 'You mustn't think I've been idle this past week. Ever since I received de Baudicourt's note that she was on her way I've been making enquiries. The girl's from a respectable family all right, but there was some trouble over a broken marriage contract last year. Some young fellow threatened a breach of promise action. And she left her home without permission. De Tremouille told me that her parents are nearly out of their minds with worry, and too frightened to oppose de Baudicourt who has this crazy notion that she might be genuine.'

'Even if she isn't, it might be amusing,' Agnes said, swiftly changing her tactics.

'And God knows we could do with a little amusement,' the Dauphin agreed.

'Then you will see her?'

'Is she still outside the Palace?'

'You know she's waited outside the gates all day and every day since she arrived at Chinon! I've been trying to get a good look at her from the windows, but she keeps her head down. Can I tell d'Alençon that you'll let her in?'

'Provided we apply the test.' Charles bit off another grape and patted his sweetheart's rounded posterior as she hurried by.

An hour later, Agnes stood with the other Court ladies in the great candlelit hall of the Palace.

Others, she thought, might take life in palaces for granted, but she, sprung from low beginnings, never ceased to marvel at the luxury and colour amid which her life was spent. The Dauphin might be poor in comparison with other monarchs, but in comparison to the lot of his subjects, his life was a wild dream of extravagance.

She smoothed her blue velvet gown over her hips and turned her head so that she could enjoy the caress of her lace veil as it brushed her cheek. The fact that the gown had not yet been paid for, and the lace was a present from the Dauphine, never troubled her thoughts. It was perfectly possible to enjoy the good things of life without conscience. Then she spotted the Dauphin standing among the retainers, and remembered the royal debts.

Dear, foolish, troubled Charles! How she loved him and how she despised him! In her loving there was a feeling of impatient contempt; and in her despising there was great tenderness. The two were bound together, just like the splendour of the courtiers and the poverty of the crown. They were the pattern of her life.

'You look very serious, my dear Agnes!' D'Alençon had entered and was smiling at her. Sometimes Agnes thought that, if she were not so entirely committed to the Dauphin, she might have fallen in love with the handsome young duke. He had married the Dauphin's cousin and his devotion to his pretty wife was so excessive that it might have been amusing to tempt him into unfaithfulness.

'I was hoping you would come over and talk to me,' she said, untruthfully. 'The Dauphin neglects me so shamefully that I am thinking of taking another lover.'

'And if I were not married, how quickly I would seize my opportunity!' he said, gallantly.

'It's unnatural,' she said, only half-joking, 'for such a comely man to have no mistress. You cannot mean to remain faithful to the Duchess for the rest of your married life!'

'That was what I promised when we wed!'

'Oh, the marriage vows!' She shrugged and pouted up at him. 'Nobody takes them seriously any more. The Dauphin doesn't!'

'Charles takes very little seriously,' d'Alençon smiled, 'but I have dull, old-fashioned notions. When I talk to you, my sweet Agnes, I wish my conscience confined me less. But even if it did, you would not have me, you know. You too are faithful.'

'To Charles? I suppose I am. I can't think why. He's obstinate, and weak, and needs to be bossed and bullied, and scolded and nagged.'

'And that is why you love him,' d'Alençon said, affectionately, and kissed her hand.

There was a buzz of excited chatter around them as the great doors opened. The figure in royal robes sat stiffly on the high dais, and even Madame de Treues, who prided herself on her deportment, thrust forward her shoulder and craned her neck.

The girl looked quite small, thought Agnes, as she stood framed in the archway, with the spears of the men-at-arms dwarfing her. She appeared stocky, and squat, oddly foreshortened. There were a few, hastily-stifled titters as the crowd took in her short hair and neat black suit. The only touch of colour in her costume was the red feather pushed into her cap. It was a jaunty little feather, and for some reason it struck Agnes as faintly pathetic, as if the odd little creature had attempted to remind people that it was a female.

Then, amid the curious stares and muffled whispers, the visitor spoke.

'I beg you not to deceive me,' she said, and her voice was startlingly sweet.

She was walking towards the dais, and Agnes dug her nails into her palms, willing the trick to be unsuccessful.

At the foot of the steps, the girl hesitated. Then she turned away, with an impatient gesture and began to walk slowly up and down the rows of assembled courtiers.

She had reached Agnes now, and close to, it was possible to see the beads of sweat on her face. Her dark gaze flicked indifferently past the royal mistress, rested briefly on d'Alençon and then she had moved on, and was pushing her way past de Baudicourt, and curtseying before the Dauphin.

'I am Joan, La Pucelle,' rang out her voice. 'The King of Heaven sends me to you with the message that you shall be crowned and annointed as King of France in the city of Rheims.'

Even at that moment, Agnes saw, the Dauphin was still irresolute. He backed a pace or two, waving an arm feebly in the general direction of de Tremouille.

'There stands the real Dauphin,' he said.

'In God's name, noble prince, it is you and none other!' came Joan's voice again.

Charles blinked, swallowed, then extended a limp hand to be kissed.

'It's a miracle! It's a real miracle!' Agnes breathed.

'She has certainly passed the test,' d'Alençon murmured.

His face was alight with interest, and Agnes felt his own excitement match with hers.

The Dauphin was pulling off his concealing cloak and leading Joan to the inner room. De Tremouille was gnawing his lip sulkily, and the murmurs were rising to exclamations.

Several of the ladies were declaring they had never seen anything so comical as the girl who aped a man, although Madame de Baudicourt was shaking her horned head-dress from side to side.

'For my part,' she cried, 'I never wish to see anything so scandalously outlandish again in my life!'

All was bustle and chatter, and witty comment, but Agnes had the curious feeling that in an instant everything would vanish. The ladies and noblemen in their stiff, fantastic clothes—why should she see these lovely garments as fantastic?—would crumble, and the stone walls would dissolve, and there would be green grass where now there were carpets.

'And we will all be forgotten, except for her,' she said, aloud.

'Are you all right, Madame?'

The room swung back into focus and her unsteadiness was gone. She linked her fingers with d'Alençon, laughed merrily, and countered his anxious enquiry with a request for some wine.

It was very late when the Dauphin visited her that night, and by the time he came, Agnes was in a thoroughly bad temper. The palace was seething with rumour and counter-rumour, and she, who was usually at the centre of affairs, knew no more than anybody else.

Charles had remained closeted with Joan for hours; then de Tremouille and d'Alençon had been called to the private room. They had eaten supper there together and Agnes had hurried to her room to change her dress. But nobody had sent for her, or offered to present her formally to the girl from Domremy.

'I hope you don't forget that it was I who persuaded you to see the maid,' she began tartly, as the Dauphin entered.

'She is certainly an astonishing creature,' the Dauphin agreed.

His sallow complexion was flushed and he looked unusually animated.

'She recognized you among all the others,' Agnes marvelled. 'What did she say to you when you were alone? We were all consumed with curiosity.'

'She lectured me,' Charles admitted, 'on my duty to God, my duty to my Kingdom, and my duty to myself.'

'Why, that's nothing,' Agnes said disappointed, 'for I'm always lecturing you.'

'But you never repeated to me word for word my most secret prayers.'

'Did she do that?'

'That and more. She can read the past and the future, and see into the nature of things more deeply than anyone I ever met. She told me that she had heard voices since she was a child, instructing her and guiding her. And the Archangel Michael and the saints Catherine and Margaret come down to her. She told me so many odd things that I can't recall the half of them. But she has some great power working in her, I'm sure.'

'Will you let her ride with the army?' Agnes asked, curiously.

'If d'Alençon had his way, she'd be commanding my battalions already,' the Dauphin grinned. 'I never saw him so taken with anybody since he met his wife. He and La Pucelle were teasing each other like old friends before the meal was over.'

'La Pucelle—the virgin?' Agnes mused. 'It's a proud title.'

'Are you jealous, my love?'

'Curious, let us say. I wish I could meet this pucelle. I mean, really meet and talk with her.'

'She is more interested in meeting my knights and captains,' said the Dauphin.

His lips twitched as he remembered the pucelle's crisp refusal when he had offered to introduce her to his mistress.

'I will be happy to meet the Dauphine Marie, but I have no time to waste on whores.'

'And de Tremouille? He won't like her, I'll be bound!'

'They were polite,' Charles said, 'but they eyed each other like fighting cocks. De Tremouille has counselled patience. He advises me to wait and have the girl investigated fully. Joan wants me to send her off to Orleans at once. She intends to begin her campaign by raising the seige, if you please. She seems completely confident that she can do it, too.'

'She has evidently given you some confidence,' Agnes said, approvingly.

'And that is what interests me,' Charles said, eagerly. 'While one is talking to her one feels it might be possible to conquer the whole world. If she can make one man feel like that, what might she not do with a whole army? She might be just what is needed to restore morale. D'Alençon thinks so. Why, under her inspiration, we might even win a few victories! Then, if we had some success behind us, we could come to terms with the Anglo-Burgundian alliance.'

'Is that what Joan wants?'

'Oh, her ideas are much more ambitious.' Charles threw himself on the bed and drew Agnes into his arms. 'She wants to drive every Englishman back to England and every Burgundian back to Burgundy, and unite France under one crown. It's a great scheme, but quite impractical in this day and age. These peasants don't understand the finer points of diplomacy.'

'But if she has power?'

'We will allow her to use that power,' Charles said grandly. 'This pucelle may be the most useful weapon with which I've ever been provided.'

'I beg you not to deceive me,' Agnes murmured, remembering that stocky figure with a feather in her hat.

The Dauphin was undoing her bodice and merely grunted in reply, but Agnes shivered with an unexplained pity before submitting to her lover with less than her usual enthusiasm.

Joan had lost her temper again. She paced up and down the room of her lodgings, striking the fist of one hand into the palm of the other while she poured out into the air a string of grievances.

Huddled on his pallet in the corner, Minguet watched her with his mouth half-open. The fourteen-year-old boy had been living in a daze since the day, a month before, when his overlord, the Seigneur de Baudicourt, had informed him he was to act as page to the virgin from Lorraine. The idea of having to wait upon a girl had seemed attractive, for ladies usually spoke gently and made a fuss of one.

This girl was not, however, in the usual run of ladies. Joan never ruffled his hair or fed him sweetmeats or told him he was a sweet lad. Instead she scolded him for being greedy, boxed his ears when she caught his attention wandering during Vespers, called him 'Wretch', and poured out a string of complaints every time she glanced in his direction. Minguet was terrified of her, fascinated by her, and would have died for her at any moment.

'Cowgirl!' Joan was raging. 'Cowgirl! Those goddams *insulted* me! They stood and laughed when I told them to go back to the country God had given them. I couldn't believe that even Englishmen could be so stupid! And close your mouth, Minguet! If you go about with it hanging open, you're liable to catch flies! It's not as if I hadn't warned them before! I dictated a letter to the Duke of Bedford that should have sent him scuttling back over the sea. I am the most patient person in the world, but there is a limit to what even I can stand!'

Joan had, she felt, ample reason for her annoyance. She had fully expected that when the Dauphin had seen her, he would immediately allow her to join the army at

Orleans. Instead she had been taken to Tours where a bevy of ladies had examined her so minutely that Joan's cheeks burned when she remembered the humiliation. From Tours they had taken her to Poitiers where a Council of churchmen had questioned her for hours. Then it was back to Chinon, where they had fitted her out with armour and painted a banner according to her directions.

She had asked them to dig up the sword that St Michael had left for her behind the altar of St Catherine at Fierbois. Everybody had seemed very surprised to discover that such a sword was actually found in the place she had directed.

People, thought Joan, were so stupid! They could not accept what God sent without testing it; they could not recognize the truth without questioning it. Then she relaxed a little and smiled, because not all people had been so foolish. While the princes and prelates argued and examined, the common people had flocked in crowds to see her. They had massed about the walls of the castle and shouted for her over and over, until she had come out to the battlements and showed herself in armour, with her battle-axe in her hand.

And, at last, the Dauphin had drawn up letters patent which allowed her to ride with the soldiers; but even then the captains had cheated her. They had not ridden to Orleans along the northern route where they could have entered the town through the supply gates. Instead, they had brought her in a wide arc to the south, so that the river lay between her troops and the town.

'The town is almost completely surrounded by the English forces,' Gilles de Raiz explained, when she had indignantly demanded some reason for the detour. 'If you will look at the map, Joan, you will see that they hold the Bastille de St Pouair and the Bastille de Pressoir Airs on the north; on the west they block the river at L'ile de Charlemagne and at the Bastille de St Laurent; on the east they hold the Bastille de St Loup and the Bastille de St Jean le Blanc; on the south—'

'What is the use of pushing documents in my face when you know I can't tell A from B,' Joan cried, irritably. 'And are there no goddams on the south?'

'The English hold the Tourelles across the river, but their forts on the south are smaller and more widely spaced. We can ferry across the Loire at Checy.'

At Checy there had been another delay, for the waters had raged sullenly under a windswept sky, and it was impossible to launch the boats. It had been the captain's turn to fume and fret, and Joan's turn to counsel patience because sooner or later the wind would change. And the wind did change, so suddenly, that everybody declared it was a miracle.

Even when Joan had entered the town, having crossed the river without hindrance, she had been forced to leave the main body of her troops behind. Count Dunois had come out personally to escort her through the gates, but she was too tired and disappointed to bother to be polite. It was of no use for the pleasant-faced Governor to assure her there were too many soldiers to bring safely across the Loire and too few of them to launch a successful attack against the English. It was of no use for the citizens to rush out bearing torches, crying that their deliverer had come. Joan could only remember the ranks of men drawn up in the pouring rain along the banks of the river. She had brought them to Orleans, promised them a victory over the goddams, and the captains refused to give the order to attack.

She had used the delay in the only way she could imagine might be some use—by dictating furious demands to the leaders of the English to withdraw and by inspecting the fortifications.

Dressed in her armour, Joan had clambered up and down flights of stone steps, shook hands with soldiers who proudly showed her their cannons and guns, and tried to look extremely intelligent when Dunois spread out maps before her.

She had made a good impression upon the citizens, she knew. They followed her wherever she went, holding up their children to her, calling her their own pucelle.

'And I have done nothing yet!' she cried, angrily. 'I have accomplished nothing. I went out to the bridge and called upon them to leave, and they laughed at me!'

She had been deeply humiliated by that laughter, bubbling up from a hundred English throats. They had not even bothered to aim an arrow at her, although she had been expecting a whole flight of them when she strode on to the bridge. And, although she had no fear of death, her voices had told her she would be wounded at Orleans.

But there had been no wound except the mocking cries of 'Cowgirl!' and pity in Dunois's eyes when she came back into the town.

She broke off in her angry pacing and listened intently. Then her face cleared and she gripped Minguet's shoulder, hauling him to his feet.

'Marching feet!' she exclaimed, and gave him a comradely hug. 'Can you hear that tramp—tramp—tramp up and down the streets and alleys? Can you hear those voices? French voices, boy! The reinforcements have arrived. Dunois told me he had sent for more troops and they are here. They're pouring in! And by tonight de Raiz will be here from Blois!'

She gave him a good-natured shake, laughing down into his face.

'We must go out and welcome them. They are my soldiers, come to fight for France. And close your mouth, child, before you completely forget your manners!'

By mid-afternoon the town was in a fever of excitement. Soldiers were crammed at every wall, and every citizen undertook to lodge a dozen or so. The great cannon, Rifflard, was mounted on the main turret and seventy-one smaller cannon poked their sinister snouts over the battlements. At every corner, axes and lances, maces and culverins were neatly stacked.

The streets throbbed with life. Women with children clinging wide-eyed to their skirts distributed soup to men who spoke in the dialects of many provinces. The men who had escorted Joan to Orleans had returned from Blois and formed a tight circle around the house of the lieutenant, d'Aulun, within which Joan was resting. Other men were still coming into Orleans along the northern supply route. Soldiers from Gien, Montargis, Chateau Reynard and Chateaudun were mingling with those already there. And from mouth to mouth the whisper ran, 'The Maid will lead us to victory. This time there will be a victory!'

In the lieutenant's house, the captains sat gloomily about the table. Only d'Alençon's handsome face bore any signs of confidence.

'You are young,' grumbled La Hire, 'but I am past thirty and have seen more battles. Half these 'reinforcements' are untrained, unarmed, and without sense. One volley from the goddams, and they'll drop their breeches and run like the devil.'

'Have you no faith in our great fighting men?' Gilles de Raiz asked.

'These are not men! These are bloody farmhands, and bleeding schoolboys,' La Hire exploded. 'I am a Gascon, of Gascony. Let me have a dozen Gascons and we'll drive the sodding goddams into the channel.'

'If Joan wakes up and hears you swearing like that,' de Poulengy remarked 'then you'll be the one driven into the channel.'

The tension relaxed as a general chuckle ran around the table.

La Hire grinned sheepishly and rubbed his chin.

'I can't open my mouth without throwing an oath out,' he admitted, 'but I'm a plain-spoken man. I told that to the Maid. "I'm a plain-spoken man," I said, "and my business is fighting, not making pretty speeches." And do you know what she said to me? She said, "If you fight on God's side, you must use godly language. If you *must* swear, say 'in the name of the Lord', and thus an oath becomes a gentle one." '

'Tell them what happened next,' prompted de Metz.

'I went to Confession,' La Hire said, lookng, if it were possible, even more sheepish. 'That girl informed me that I must confess my sins, and blast me! I mean, in the name of God, there I was, trotting off to church like a lamb to the slaughter.'

'And very soon we may all be trotting off to battle with the like result,' Dunois observed.

'The English are more sensible than we are,' shrugged de Raiz. 'They sit quietly in their circle of fortresses and laugh into their ale because they know we have neither the men nor the guns to attack in every direction at once.'

'But soon we must attack!' D'Alençon cried. 'I have not travelled here to sit and gossip with a group of old friends. My wife didn't want me to ride to battle again, but I came because the Maid assured me that there would be a great victory. How can there be a victory if there is no battle?'

'The Duke puts us to shame,' Dunois said. 'He has reminded us of our duty and the glory that waits to be won. We must sally out and take the Bastille de St Loup.'

'Just sally out and take it,' yawned d'Aulun. 'Before or after supper, my dear Dunois?'

'The Bastille de St Loup is less well-defended than the other forts. It is the weak link in the chain,' Dunois said, earnestly. 'You all know that Sir John Fastolf is on his way to St Loup. It would be to our advantage if his force were intercepted before it reached St Loup.'

'Then we must tell Joan what we intend!'

'For Heaven's sake, d'Alençon! Have you learnt no better sense than that?' Dunois pressed the younger man back into his seat. 'Ever since the Maid arrived she has countermanded my orders, altered the existing arrangements, turned my entire household upside down. She has scarcely laid down for the past four nights. Last night she was on her knees until dawn. She woke up her page three times and ordered him to pray with her. Do you think she could possibly be of any use in a battle? It will be difficult enough for seasoned warriors, but for a young girl who has never seen blood spilt, it would be impossible. We could not hope to protect her.'

'But she is La Pucelle, sent by God,' de Poulengy argued.

'And do you think God would be pleased with us if we exposed the holy maiden to danger?' Dunois asked. 'I believe that she is holy, and we cannot risk the loss of so precious a charge.'

The others nodded gravely and instinctively lowered their voices as they speedily planned their formations and agreed that d'Aulun, to that gentleman's secret relief, must remain within the town in order to maintain a possible way of retreat.

From rank to rank the whisper went, and men who had milled around the gates and alleys straightened up, grim-faced and silent to follow the banners of their leige lords.

Joan, woken by the tramping of feet under her window, was half-way to the door when consciousness of the external world faded and she was caught up in the light, surrounded by the voices.

When the voices faded and the room swam into focus again, she was confused and angry. D'Aulun, who had put up his feet in expectation of a brief doze, was shaken awake by a furiously indignant pucelle.

'In the name of God, my voices have told me to go against the goddams,' she exclaimed, 'but I don't know whether I am to go against their forts or against Fastolf and his supply train. I need to consult with my captains and there is no sign of them.'

'The attack has begun, Joan,' the lieutenant said soothingly.

'Begun? Without me? Was that the meaning of the

marching feet? They delay me for days and then they leave me sleeping and sneak out to attack!'

'But you didn't mean to go actually into battle,' d'Aulun began feebly.

'Who are you to tell me what I meant to do!' Joan exploded. 'Did you think I would sit indoors with my weaving while everybody else did the work and took the risks? Where are the people whose business it is to arm me! Minguet! In the name of God, rub the sleep out of your eyes and get my horse. You, d'Aulun, round up all the remaining soldiers and order them to follow me.'

'But they must guard the line of retreat.'

'There will be no retreat! Marshall the soldiers. And get hold of Father Pacquerel. I need his blessing before I ride out. You, little girl,' she grabbed at one of the lieutenant's daughters who was peeping around the door, 'come upstairs and help me to put on my armour. D'Aulun! Why are you still here?'

All was confusion. Struggling into her armour, hearing shouts and running feet and the distant booming of cannon, Joan was conscious of an overwhelming haste that drove her on.

Finally encased in her suit, with the round metal cap pulled firmly over her head, she knelt briefly as Father Pacquerel entered the room, then clattered downstairs.

'My banner!' she gasped as she was hoisted to the high pommel. 'Minguet! Fetch my banner! In the name of God, stir yourself, wretch! Do you think I want to sit here all day? Are these all the men left in Orleans? No matter! They will not be cheated out of their share of fighting. D'Aulun, unless you intend to stroll to the battle, get on your horse! Get that little girl out of the way before the hoofs crush her! Will somebody have the sense to open the gate?'

They were streaming through the gate, a motley band of cavalry and foot soldiers with d'Aulun cursing as he tried to mount his horse unaided, with women screeching as stones flew up into their inquisitive faces, and the energetic young figure urging them forward.

At one moment, it seemed, they were back in the town. At the next they were caught up in a dense, swaying mass of men locked in hand to hand combat while around them hailed stones and arrows and flame-tipped faggots. Everywhere was the high-pitched screaming of horses, the deep grunting breath of men fighting for their lives, and underfoot a ground already slimy with blood and entrails.

Almost impossible to tell friend from foe, for distinguishing badges were muddied and obscure. Joan raised herself in the stirrups, handed the banner to Minguet who rode his own pony, drew her sword from its sheath and heard her own voice ring out, triumphant and strong.

'Go on, in the name of France and the Maid, for the Glory of God!'

Her words were taken up by those nearest to her, and men wiping sweat from their eyes, seeing the figure on horseback magnified by their own hopes, charged again and again, driving back the English in a confusion of blood and battle-axe, arrows, culverins, spiked cannon-balls and stabbing lances.

When twilight drifted down over the land, the last rays of the sun picked out the littered bodies, some lying still, others moving in the groping, womb gestures of the dying. The banks of the river were thick with discarded weapons and horses vainly trying to find a foothold in the mud.

Over the Bastille de St Loup fluttered the French banners, and from the direction of Orleans came the joyful peals of bells.

D'Alençon pushed back his helmet and wiped his dripping sword across the heaving flanks of his horse.

'A victory!' he enthused. 'Can you believe it, Dunois? A French victory!'

'The first of many, if the signs be right!' Dunois grinned back cheerfully.

'We were fools to imagine Joan would not ride out to

take part!' exclaimed d'Aulun. 'She may take all the credit she desires, for I swear the men fought like tigers when they saw her riding in.'

'If one English fort can be taken, so can all the rest,' shouted La Hire.

He had pulled off his helmet entirely and blood streaming from a cut over his eyebrow gave him an even more rakish appearance than usual.

He wheeled his horse away from the little group and cantered over to where Joan sat some distance away. Behind her, Minguet still hovered, excitement all over his round, freckled face. It had been his first battle and now that it was over, and he found himself, surprisingly, in one piece, he was beginning to forget he had ever been afraid.

He was puzzled, however, by Joan's quietness and stillness. Throughout the engagement she had been everywhere, brandishing her sword and shouting above the din and confusion. And the fort had been taken; the goddams driven back. In Joan's place he would have been jumping for joy, but the Maid had not spoken one word since the fleur-de-lys had been run up the flagpole of the Bastille de Loup.

She drooped in the saddle as if she were immensely weary, and her face was still and shadowed.

'A fine victory, Pucelle!' La Hire called out. 'You must be very proud.'

'Proud?' She echoed the word flatly, turning tear-blurred eyes towards him. 'What cause is there for pride in all this? How can there be a fine victory when so many are dead? They never told me that it would be like this. I thought only of winning the fight.'

'To win the fight one has to kill the enemy,' La Hire said, reasonably.

'And when the enemy is dead, it is possible to look at him and see that he is just a man,' she answered, and began to sob in a kind of tired anguish. 'All these English are just men, Captain. Most of them are here because their captains have ordered them to be here. If I could have talked to them—really talked to them—they might all have decided to go back to their own country. And they're so young, La Hire. They ought to have lived longer and died quietly. Perhaps some of them died with their sins unconfessed. It tortures me to imagine their souls going to hell because I never gave them time to repent their sins! Oh, I wish I were at home again. I wish I were back at Domremy!'

La Hire bit his lip in perplexity. It was useless to assure Joan that she was suffering from the sort of battle fatigue that made grown men sit down and cry for their mothers when the danger was past. In a moment she was liable to have a most unwarlike attack of hysterics.

'They're not all dead, Pucelle,' he said, hastily. 'What do you want us to do with the wounded? We can send for the priests to hear confessions now, if you like.'

'Oh, yes! Yes! She rubbed her fists into her eyelids and straightened up. 'We must *all* confess! Every man must confess before he goes into battle again. And the wounded must be tended. They must be carried into the Bastille, and most gently treated.'

'And the prisoners? There are half a hundred of them.'

'They must be given food and water,' she declared. 'And there must be no looting. We are not here to steal.'

'And when do we attack again?'

'Tomorrow is Ascension Day. We can't fight on Ascension Day. It will be a day of thanksgiving!'

'The goddams will have time to redeploy their bloody forces!' La Hire expostulated.

'Don't swear!'

He could tell by the irritation in her tone that she was fast regaining her composure.

'I'll dictate another letter to the goddams,' she declared. 'It will be a very short, very warlike note. If they have any sense they'll pay heed to it. If not, then we'll attack again the day after tomorrow.'

She swung round abruptly and, leaning over, caught

Minguet by his ear.

'Little wretch, to go charging grown men at your age!' she scolded. 'You thought I wouldn't notice you, but I saw you riding against the enemy. Would you believe it, La Hire, but this child managed himself like a seasoned trooper? Now you must ride with me, boy, back to Orleans. We will enter the gates together, but in the name of God, brat, close your mouth first!'

Rubbing his smarting ear and trotting obediently behind his mistress, Minguet had never been so happy in his life.

CHAPTER SIX

ORLEANS, MAY, 1429

O N the day following the next, the soldiers of France rode
out again, led by the odd armoured figure with her standard
in her hand. They rode in a wide arc, sweeping to the
south-east towards the Bastille de St Jean le Blanc. The
fort was deserted, however, save for two weeping page-
boys left behind in the general confusion, who declared in
execrable French that their own people had withdrawn to
the Bastille des Augustins.

The French turned westward, some riding along the
banks of the river while the foot-soldiers crossed the water
to join up with the main cavalry.

'A brave sight!' commented La Hire, but the girl at his
side only nodded briefly.

The woman who two days before had wept for the
souls of her fallen enemies, was now the stern young captain with her eyes fixed firmly on conquest.

A volley of cannon-balls met them as the gates of des
Augustins came into view. There was sudden panic as men
were tumbled from their horses, and others, caught in the
melee, crushed and mangled by flying hoofs.

From his position in the rear, d'Aulun heard the trumpets
sound the retreat, and had almost wheeled his mount
around when he became aware that, despite the signal, the
troops were still advancing. And ahead of them, half-
standing in the saddle, Joan rode furiously, her lance un-
couched, while by her side, La Hire struggled desperately
to maintain his grip on his own horse and lance, and the
standard the Maid had thrust at him.

Another volley of cannon! Men crouched under their
wooden pavas like tortoises, as they shoved forward the
bulky battering rams. Arrows were falling like rain, and

across the ground rolled the deadly chausse-trappes, those iron balls whose vicious spikes could lame a horse or trip a running man.

There was no sign of Joan, and for a moment, d'Aulun's heart faltered. Then he saw her, on foot, urging some youths who were dragging forward the scaling-ladders. She looked, he noticed incredulously, as if she were enjoying herself immensely.

A clanging of iron and a splintering of wood, flames licking the edges of the grass, a man tumbling backwards beneath the slash of a battle-axe, and in all the confusion, the English streaming away from the fort, leaving their wounded and dead, and the lilies of France waving over the towers. Such were d'Aulun's jumbled impressions, as he gained the shelter of the outer bailey and saw Joan again. She was leaning against the wall, wiping grime from her face with one hand, and tenderly rubbing her unbooted foot with the other.

'A chausse-trappe,' she said, ruefully, 'it spiked me when I fell off my horse. And you may take that grin off your face, d'Aulun, for I was not reared to ride war horses in the midst of battle.'

'Will you follow the English again today?' La Hire enquired, leading up Joan's horse.

'We have chased them to Les Tourelles,' Joan said, 'and we won't grudge them a night's rest before we harry them further. Now we'll go back to the town and take Council there.'

It was a stormy Council that night. Listening to them, Joan wondered, fleetingly, if it would ever be possible to turn into reality the dream of a united France when even her leaders could not agree.

D'Alençon was, as usual, on the side of the angels. He was ready to follow Joan all the way across the Channel to the capital of the English King himself if she thought it necessary. Under cover of the general argument, he was writing to his wife, assuring her that he was well and unharmed and loved her truly.

At the other end of the table, the Marshal de Raiz and the Marshal de Sainte-Severe were declaring furiously that they were not cowards, but neither were they fools! And to attack Les Tourelles where the goddams were firmly entrenched was suicidal.

La Hire had suggested that it might be an excellent feint to move northward against the Bastille de Saint Pouair. The baron de Coulonces had asked him how he proposed trying to sneak three thousand men through the unwooded pasture around the fort, and La Hire had angrily demanded satisfaction for the slight to his intelligence.

Dunois attempted to restore order by suggesting that they delay the attack until reinforcements could be sent from Blois, and that meanwhile scouts should go out in search of Fastolf's men who must be somewhere in the area.

This brought further protests from d'Alençon, who broke off in the midst of a tender passage, to cry indignantly that if they had to depend on fresh troops from Blois, they might as well surrender at once.

He turned to where Joan sat, and hotly demanded what she thought of such council.

It was strange, Dunois considered, how all the squabbling voices died away as Joan stood up. She was no very heroic figure at that moment, with her hair plastered in greasy locks around her face and her sore foot tied up in a scarf, but there was the usual confidence in her tone.

'I have already taken counsel with my voices,' she said, firmly, 'and my counsel is better than yours. We will attack Les Tourelles tomorrow at dawn. Whoever holds that fort on the river holds Orleans. So we will take Les Tourelles.'

'We would do better to bypass it and either go north to the Bastille de Saint Pouair or continue westward to the Bastille du Champ de Saint Prive,' Dunois began.

'And take a week, perhaps a month, to storm one bastille

after another, when we might win all on one decisive thrust!'

'Sometimes it's best to hasten slowly, Pucelle,' d'Aulun said.

'This is not such a time,' she answered. 'Why do you sit about, trying to decide what to do when I am here for that purpose? Don't any of you understand my mission yet? Do you think me a little carrot to be dangled before the noses of the soldiers when they are reluctant to go forward, and locked up in the cupboard like a dumb vegetable when there are matters to be discussed?'

'Child, we know you have great faith, and we have faith in you,' Dunois said, kindly, 'but these are practical matters.'

'Do you think God isn't practical?' Joan asked. 'Do you think that it is my power that has brought you these victories and will bring you even greater victories? I am the straw through which God blows His Grace. So you will follow me, not because I know more about fighting than you know, but because I know the will of God!'

Dunois flung up his hands in an expressive gesture, and spoke with amused resignation.

'What do you want us to do, Joan?'

'Every man must go to confession again tonight,' she declared, ignoring a stifled groan from La Hire. 'All the loose women in the town must be sent away at once, so that those who are fated to die tomorrow, will spend their last night in a way pleasing to God. And we must rise very early, earlier than we did today.'

'And you will ride with us?'

'Tomorrow I will have more work to do than I have ever done, and blood will flow from my body above my breast. My voices have told me of it.'

When she had finished, there was deep silence, and even La Hire felt a cold chill for when the Maid spoke and looked in such a fashion, there was nothing for an ordinary man to add.

At first light, Joan knelt, booted and spurred, before the portable altar set up in the main square so that the whole army might hear Mass. Then she was hoisted to her mount while the soldiers filed past, some saluting, others touching her foot with the tips of their fingers.

'Won't you eat something before you leave?'

She smiled down at Jacques Boucher, who was holding up a trout in a dish.

'In the name of God, we will eat it for supper,' she answered, cheerfully, 'when we will bring back a goddam to eat his share.'

There was a howl of delight from those who heard her words, and then the gates were opened and the cavalcade left the town, marching and riding down to the banks of the Loire.

'Has the Maid given any orders for the plan of attack?' de Raiz enquired.

'She has ordered us merely to go forward,' Dunois shrugged. 'But the task will be more difficult than she or the men realize. I think she expects the goddams to run away when they see her coming.'

'At least they don't call her Cow-girl any longer!' de Raiz grinned. 'It's amazing how that upset her, but peasants have such an exaggerated sense of social barriers!'

There was no more time for conversation. There was no more time for anything, because salvoes of fire were already issuing from the mouths of the cannon, and two boats, piled high with ammunition, had capsized.

Minguet, his face shining with excitement, had flung himself and his pony into the place where he had last seen the Maid. In battle he tried to stay as close behind her as possible, although sometimes it was difficult for she seemed to be everywhere at once.

At one moment, she was at the foot of a scaling-ladder, calling to men to follow her. At the next instant she had paused to exchange quips with a couple of archers who were boasting loudly of their skill. Then she was riding pell-mell to the very edge of the fosse, shouting for victory, with her battle-axe whirling about her head. So far, she had escaped unhurt, but today she was to be wounded. Minguet was quite sure that if Joan said she would be hurt in battle then it would happen, but he had every intention of staying near, with some confused idea of rushing forward at the last minute and saving her.

But the hours passed, and although he saw her standard fluttering, now near at hand, and now in the distance, there were too many slashing, hacking soldiers between. His arm ached from the heaviness of his sword, and the muscles of his legs throbbed with tension.

He longed to perform some brave deed that would bring Joan cantering back to his side, perhaps to praise him or call him 'wretch', but beyond cutting his own pathway across the field there was nothing much for him to do. The English ignored him even though he rode, shouting for the Maid, right up to one tall axeman. The man merely grinned, shoved him aside and went in search of bigger prey.

Dispirited and tired, Minguet rode away to the edge of the clearing and wished he were six inches taller or ten years older.

'If you seek the Maid,' d'Alençon shouted, 'she has been carried from the field. An arrow pierced her above the left breast.'

He might have said more, but Minguet spurred his pony in the direction the Duke had pointed.

Joan was propped up in the shade of a hedge some distance from the main battlefield. Two physicians had just finished bandaging her wound, and the Sieur de Gamaches was sponging her face.

There were at least a dozen men kneeling around her, and at the side Father Pacquerel was intoning his prayers with an expression of sepulchral gloom on his rather heavy face.

'Let me pass! Oh, please, let me pass!'

Minguet slipped from the saddle and tried to push his way past La Hire, who was cursing, fluently and without taking breath.

'Is that Minguet? Let him come!' Joan had struggled into a sitting position. Although her face was extremely white, her voice sounded reassuringly normal.

'Are you hurt badly, Pucelle? You're not going to *die*, are you?'

'Of course not, silly boy! The wound is a flesh wound only, and the bleeding has quite stopped.'

'We dressed it with olive oil and lard,' said one of the physicians, deferentially.

'Now, if you have rested a little, we can call the stretcher-bearers,' said the other.

'Stretcher-bearers!' Joan's voice shrilled with indignation. 'Stretcher-bearers! Do you think I will allow you to carry me back to Orleans on a stretcher? Before the day is over, I intend to ride back into the conflict! You may inform the captains so! And what in the world are you men doing on your knees? Do you think that is the way to beat the goddams! La Hire, get back to your men! Gentlemen, there are others who need your services more than I do. Minguet, you will not be afraid to stand guard over me while I rest, will you?'

But, by mid-afternoon, Joan was on her feet again, shaky and pale, but loudly demanding to be rearmed and re-mounted.

She had scarcely been assisted to her horse when Dunois rode up, with Gilles de Raiz close behind.

'Pucelle! We cannot possibly storm Les Tourelles today. We must sound the retreat and leave the field. We can sally out again tomorrow.'

'Give me fifteen minutes. I want to pray.'

'But, Joan—'

'Fifteen minutes!' she repeated, firmly, and galloped away to a neighbouring vineyard.

'She has gone to speak with her voices,' Minguet said in hushed tones.

'Can they tell her how to make exhausted men stand on their feet again?' de Raiz wondered, cynically.

'There will be a victory, if the Pucelle says so,' muttered Minguet, resentfully.

He disliked de Raiz with his long fingers and glittering eyes, and kept out of his way as much as possible.

Joan was back within ten minutes and the look on her face was exultant.

'Sound a general attack!' she yelled over her shoulder as she galloped past.

'The girl's out of her mind,' de Raiz said helplessly.

Indeed, it seemed as if Joan had taken complete leave of her senses. She was streaking past the groups still locked in half-hearted combat, past the dead and the dying and the ministering priests. She was riding to the very parapet of the deep fosse, and there, standing in her saddle, holding on high her bright painted banner, she shouted, amid the smoke and thunder of cannon.

'Turn again, citizens of France. Victory in the name of God! Les Tourelles is ours to take!'

And, incredibly, it was so! Men who had already turned their backs towards the fort were rushing to stand behind Joan with their weapons unleashed. A thousand voices took up her imperious cry and flung it in the faces of the complacent enemy. Men who had believed they were too beaten to move another yard found themselves clambering up ladders, hurling faggots, leaping ditches, swarming across the bridge.

The enemy were in retreat! English archers lay like broken dolls at the foot of the high walls. Others crawled painfully over the twisted wreckage of their culverins and cannons.

The English leaders, with Sir William Glasdale at their head, were fleeing across the long bridge. Beneath its wooden struts, fireboats were being pushed by long poles, and there was a sudden blinding flash as the flames caught pitch soaked wood and exploded. The wooden bridge broke into fragments and pieces of it were flung high into the air.

Joan, triumphant on the parapet, with the cheering troops about her, broke into harsh sobbing as she saw the flames and heard the choking screams of men, helpless in their armour, dragged beneath the swirling waters of the Loire. One knight, flaming like a living torch, crashed past her, so near that she smelt his scorching flesh.

'Les Tourelles is ours!' Dunois was shouting.

'Orleans is free!' cried d'Aulun, almost hysterical with joy.

'We have won back the town for the Dauphin,' La Hire said triumphantly.

'All those poor men!' Joan said, sadly. 'Why didn't they go away as I told them to go in my letter? Why didn't they believe me? Why must there be killing before God's will is done?'

'Weep for the dead later, Joan,' de Raiz said impatiently. 'You mustn't dampen all the joy at this moment. The people of Orleans will want to welcome their deliverer.'

He had spoken half in jest, but there was no mockery in the faces of the citizens who waited to see the Pucelle ride back through the gates. Women cast only brief glances at their returning husbands and sons before rushing to hold up their children to look at Joan.

Minguet swelled with reflected pride as he heard the cheers and shouts, and the ringing of bells from the church.

Riding ahead of her captains, with the tears still flecking her lashes, Joan's head was bared under a sky still reddened by the flames from Les Tourelles.

A group of children ran out, and one of them, a flaxen-haired girl in a blue kirtle, reached up with a bunch of flowers in her hand. They were lilies—long-stemmed and fragrant, with delicate, drooping petals.

'For our Pucelle,' the girl said shyly, and there was worship in her gaze.

For a moment, Joan's eyes blurred with fresh tears. In early summer, the fields around Domremy were starred with the same pale blooms. And their faint, elusive perfume, drifting up to her nostrils, reminded her of the scent that assailed her when the heavenly ones came.

As she rode back into the town she had delivered, there was a listening look in her eyes. All around her came the shouting, cheering crowds. The citizens were heaping titles on her like garlands.

'Long live the Maid of France!'

'Blessings upon La Pucelle!'

'God bless the Maid of Orleans!'

And over and above came a new cry, beginning with a murmur and swelling to a roar.

'Long live our Joan! Long live our Joan of the lilies!'

PATAY, JUNE, 1429

Crawling through the undergrowth, Giles decided there were more congenial ways of spending a pleasant summer afternoon. The bracken was damp and green and gave out a rich, spicy scent, but he disliked the soft rustling noises around him. He disliked the crackling of twigs and the occasional patter of feet as some small woodland creature dived for cover. The thick leaves and tall trees provided ample protection, but there was nothing, in Giles's opinion, to beat a battle in the open where one could see the target. Here was the eerie sensation of too many bright eyes watching him from the cover of the thickets, and once he reared up in alarm as an adder slithered across his path.

There were documents sewn into the lining of his leather tunic and he wished heartily that he had already delivered them. It was not his job to carry messages about from one part of a forest to another, but matters were in some confusion since the evacuation from Beaugency. Men who had followed ploughs on foot in the quiet shires of Kent found themselves mounting neighing horses, and men who carried arrows and bows now carried military despatches.

The last month had been a trail of disaster. It was, thought Giles, as if one failure led to another as inevitably as one day followed another in the week. It had begun with the relief of Orleans, for Orleans had become a symbol of English strength. It had been almost ringed around by English held forts for more than six months. And then, incredibly, the harlot of Lorraine had marched into the battle and before the fortnight was up, Orleans was free.

It had been witchcraft, of course, for everybody knew that the French hadn't an ounce of courage left in them. But that defeat had demoralized the English forces, moving slowly under the command of Sir John Fastolf through the floods of a continental spring.

The English had fallen back to Meung and there watched in helpless confusion as the enemy advanced along the Loire, recapturing towns as they came and driving Talbot's forces back towards Paris.

Giles cursed his ill-luck in having chosen to serve under Fastolf, for it meant he had missed every decisive engagement. Having failed to arrive in time to help save Les Tourelles, Sir John marched his troops eastward to Jargeau, but the town fell before they arrived and news that the Duke of Suffolk himself was taken prisoner had caused a panic. The panic had grown worse when the scouts brought the news that the French had captured the bridge at Meung and were sweeping on to Beaugency.

Talbot had immediately ordered a partial evacuation to Janville, and Fastolf had hastened to join him. Perhaps it was just as well, Giles reflected sourly, for the garrison left to hold Beaugency had capitulated.

Then while the English waited for the arrival of their ally the Count of Richemont, who had promised a large force of Bretons, the same traitor Count had suddenly decided to confer with the French. And within a day all the fine, husky Bretons were wearing the fleur-de-lys and shouting for the harlot.

Now, while the English commanders discussed tactics in their comfortable quarters at Janville, hordes of exhausted men concealed themselves in the wooded plain of Patay, and wondered when the enemy would arrive.

Half the English forces were not even aware that Beaugency had been taken by the French, for communications were slow in this wooded, hilly country where it was necessary to move in small groups in order to avoid running into the enemy.

Giles was skirting the edge of a glade, and he breathed a sigh of relief as a brown-clad figure stepped out ahead and whistled softly.

'For King Henry VI,' came the password, in a cautious whisper.

'God bless the monarch of Windsor.'

Giles gave the agreed reply and judged it safe to stand up. The sentry came towards him with outstretched hand, then stopped.

'You're not Davy, the regular scout.'

'He's laid up, at the north of La Beauce, with a crushed foot. Captain Johns told me to take over,' Giles explained.

'Come on then. Lord Scales and Lord Hungerford will be eager for the despatches.'

The two noblemen seated within the tent looked, in Giles's opinion, extremely tired and thoroughly ill-humoured.

They were not in the least interested in the scout's misfortune, but snatched the package from Giles, bade him curtly to wait, and having studied the documents raised their faces in dismay.

'Do you know the drift of these messages, fellow?' Lord Hungerford asked.

'Something of them, sir. The French are approaching along the high ground, I know. And we are all scattered.'

' "Scattered" is the word!' Scales banged his fist on the

papers. 'And scatter-brained, too! Talbot orders us to march in battle-formation when the trumpets sound, but meanwhile we stay here, hiding like bush-squirrels! And Sir John Fastolf's men have not yet arrived from Meung.'

'I'm here, my lord. I came ahead, through the French lines!'

'*Your* being here makes all the difference, I suppose?' Hungerford said ironically. 'Sweet Christ! I have less than two hundred men, all tired and exceedingly hungry! This whole benighted forest is crawling with French spies. Talbot sends vague messages about trumpets, and Fastolf's troops amuse themselves by firing pot-shots at a bridge that we haven't a hope in hell of recapturing! And they send me a half-wit, to let me know what the rest of the half-wits are doing!'

'It wasn't thus in the late King's time,' Lord Scales mourned.

'Ah! for one day, with King Harry back in the saddle, instead of a pack of quarrelling curs who don't know one end of a lance from the other! You'd better get back to your troop, fellow. Tell your commander we'll hold ourselves in readiness. Can you remember that or do we have to write it down?'

'I'll remember it, sir.' Giles hastily saluted and withdrew.

When he was outside again, the sentry was waiting, with a broad grin that suggested he had heard every word.

'Bit short with you, were they? Well, it's the strain of waiting, I daresay. Gets on everybody's nerves, all the hanging around. Seen anything of the Frenchies?'

'I was trying to dodge them.'

'They say there's plenty of them around, laying ambushes and what not. Is it true the main force is on its way to the high ground?'

'Under the Duke of Alençon.'

'I've heard of him!' exclaimed the other. 'Big, handsome fellow. The pucelle's latest lover, I'm told. You know, she saved his life at Jargeau.'

'I wasn't at Jargeau.'

'Well, you didn't miss much,' the other reflected. 'It was a massacre! Mind you, the odds were against us. The d'Arc girl has all the power of the Fiend to call on. Weapons won't help against the devil.'

'She saved his life?'

'I was just coming to that! He was standing next to her and some of our fellows heard her yell to him to move; d'Alençon moved, and damn me, a second later a great chunk of stone fell on the spot where he'd been. Well, I mean, you can't fight things like that in the ordinary way. Mind you, I don't believe all the tales you hear. Some of our troops said they saw angels riding through the sky to help the French. An excuse for their own bad marksmanship, if you ask me! It stands to reason a devil-woman can't call on the aid of angels. Anyway, the right's on our side, isn't it? This country's always belonged to us. Hell's bells, we came over here with William the Conqueror in the first place!'

He broke off his narrative abruptly, one hand going to his axe while with the other he made elaborate gestures for silence.

The snapping of twigs, a soft footfall, and a young girl entered the clearing. She was evidently a gypsy, dark-skinned and black-haired with narrow, clever eyes. When she saw the two men with their axes ready, she stopped short and broke into a fluttering laugh.

'Who the devil are you?' Giles demanded.

'It's my girl,' the sentry grinned. 'There's a tribe of them somewhere in the forest, and this little beauty warms me up on guard duty. Her name's Alianor, but I can't tell you what else she says.'

'I haven't had a woman in weeks.' Giles stared longingly at the gypsy's firm golden skin and long legs.

'Then borrow her by all means. I won't grudge you ten minutes before you start back.'

Emphasizing his offer by a shove that precipitated the young woman into his companion's arms, the sentry went back to his post. Giles drew Alianor further from the tent, but when he started to push her down to the grass, she laughed again and, taking his hand, drew him further into the trees.

Ten minutes later, just as Giles was vowing to himself that, the next time he was on leave, he'd find a gypsy for himself and never lend her to anybody if she was anything like this one, the shrill blast of a hunting horn disturbed his thoughts.

There was a gap near them in the trees, and as he sat up, a fine stag bounded across the skyline. The forest, so eerily silent a moment before, was filled with cheers and shouts and the crashing of feet. Englishmen in their hundreds, spurred by the horn, dashed out from their green cover and fled up the slopes, caught by the excitement of a prospective chase; and on the heights, the French gave the signal to attack.

The screaming, yelling and clashing noises of one army slaughtering another army mingled with the indignant squawking of birds flying up from their disturbed nests and the scampering of voles and coneys.

There were shots and shouts near at hand and then the long drawn off scream of a man in mortal agony. Giles parted the bushes cautiously and saw, in the clearing where the tent had stood, a burning pyre and Milords Hungerford and Scales preparing to march off under the escort of a large soldier who wore the badge of a French captain and was swearing most horribly.

Giles had always prided himself on his cold common sense. There had been other archers in his troop who were, he admitted, more gallant and daring than he was, but most of them were dead or hopelessly crippled before they were thirty. Giles had survived because he had cultivated the art of knowing when to retreat.

Now, listening to the triumphant Gallic cheering and

the thunder of horses on the edge of the forest, and seeing that close to the burning tent was sprawled the body of the obliging sentry, Giles decided it was time to retreat again.

He had almost forgotten the girl Alianor, but she suddenly gripped his hand and pulled him away from the clearing. She seemed to know exactly where she was going although the paths twisted and turned and the branches hung low, swinging in their faces. When he remembered his own heart-stopping crawl to deliver the despatches, their present headlong course horrified him. They could so easily run into the French who seemed to be all around them. But although the shouting sometimes intensified and once a flight of arrows skimmed the earth just ahead of them, they remained incredibly alone.

They had plunged into a tunnel formed by the gnarled branches of ancient trees and were running down the arched pathway with the noises of battle fading into the distance.

Then abruptly the tunnel of trees ended and they came out by the side of a stream curving around the slopes of the hill. Alianor loosed her grip, ran to the water and plunged in up to her waist, bending and splashing the water over her head and shoulders.

Giles sat down, decided against removing his boots for fear of not getting them on again, and watched the girl. She was splashing about happily like a child, as if she had completely forgotten his existence. He wondered if she gave even one thought to her lover who lay, back in the clearing, killed by the French.

Soon, however, she came up and sat down beside him, pushing her heavy hair back while little drops of water ran down her forearms. The thin garment she wore clung wetly to her body, and her teeth were very white.

She said something in an odd, sing-song voice and pointed downstream. A soldier, with another slung across his back, was plodding towards them. It was one of Fastolf's men! Recognizing the badge, Giles hurried towards them.

The soldier eased his burden to the ground. 'Humphrey Morgan, archer in the service of Sir John Fastolf,' he panted.

Shaking hands, Giles introduced himself, and the formalities over, the new arrival launched into speech.

'Sir John is fled! If he had not fled, I would have stayed, but when I saw him riding hell for leather away from the field, I fled also. Moreover, my young brother is wounded and as this is his first taste of fighting—'

'And his last,' Giles interrupted.

The other swung around to look at the limp youngster and Giles heard him swallow convulsively.

'Your brother, you say? That's hard!'

'Hard for his poor wench when she gets the news,' the other said, bitterly. 'They'd been married less than a twelvemonth, and she begged him to stay home. But when he knew I was rejoining Fastolf, nothing would content him but he must come too.'

'And Sir John is fled?'

'Gone! Fled! Deserted! Run back to the Duke of Bedford with his tail between his legs. And we had best be on our way before we are discovered here. The Frenchies are slitting throats and asking questions afterwards. Will you help me bury my brother?'

But there was no time. The battle sounds were shifting towards them and growing louder. Giles glanced back towards Alianor but there was no sign of her. The girl had gone as if she had never existed.

The two men dragged the body to the side of the path and pulled branches down to shield it. Humphrey crossed himself and had already turned when a sudden idea seemed to strike him. Pulling out his knife, he cut a lock of hair from the head and pushed the limp, yellow strands into his pouch.

'For Margaret, his wife,' he said, half-apologetically, 'women set store by such things.'

For a moment his face was convulsed with anger and grief, and then he was striding along with Giles, as they carefully bypassed the edges of the forest and went up-stream.

'It was the deer,' Humphrey said gloomily. 'The French-ies set up a view-halloo and out we rushed, like fools! So they just cut us down as we came.'

'Did you see the whore of Lorraine?'

Humphrey shook his head.

'She was there, reciting her spells, I've no doubt. But I didn't see her. They'll blame her for all this—the Dukes, I mean—but in my opinion, it was our stupidity, not witchcraft, that made the mischief!'

'Ah, you're an educated man!'

'I had some schooling,' Humphrey admitted modestly. 'My father insisted we all learn to read and write. Even my sisters can make shift to trace their names at the end of a love-letter.'

They had come out into open country and both paused, instinctively moving back into the shelter of the trees. Other figures were hurrying across the landscape. Some ran blindly as if to escape from the horror behind them; others had linked arms around wounded comrades and made slow progress. Here and there a man had fallen and lay with open eyes gazing up into the sky. As they stood there, a boy on a horse swerved past them, shouting as he went.

'Milord Talbot is taken prisoner by the pucelle.'

His words ended abruptly and he sagged forward, with an arrow in his back.

Giles and Humphrey looked at each other in dismay.

'If Milord Talbot is made prisoner, then the sooner we make our way out of this cursed province, the better!' Giles muttered.

'We won't stand much chance, with snipers picking us off,' Humphrey mused.

'Then do we surrender?'

'To the pucelle? We do not! We turn northward and march to Paris.'

'And be shot or taken prisoner on the way?'

'Who will shoot a couple of peasants?' Humphrey enquired.

Giles grinned happily.

'I knew you were an educated man!' he exclaimed.

Five minutes later, two brown-clad figures with no distinguishing badges on their tunics plodded along the road. Their faces were grimed and they carried bundles of firewood. Now and then Giles cast a swift look at his bow, tied securely in the centre of the long branches they had hacked from the trees.

For the most part, they kept as close to the ditches as possible, with their heads down. Giles felt uncomfortably aware of his aching feet and the long miles that stretched between them and Paris.

There were others going in the same direction. A couple of Frenchmen, looking spruce and lively, galloped past, dragging a prisoner on a rope behind them. Some camp-followers, laughing wildly, had piled on to a cart and were urging their leader to hurry up. One of them had bright golden hair and had thrown a red cloak over her rags. She was kicking up her legs and calling, 'Any offers? Any offers for Bertha.'

Giles walked past, without noticing her, for his attention had been drawn to a little group ahead. An old woman, hung about with pots and pans, was urging on a younger woman carrying a baby, while a boy tried desperately to make the goat he was leading walk faster.

These were the civilians of France. These were too old, too young, too weak to fight. They cluttered the roads, blocked the escape routes, made organized fighting impossible. They were the flotsam and jetsom of a disputed land.

Now, moving slowly in their wake through the dying day, Giles felt himself to be one of them and the feeling wasn't a pleasant one.

CHAPTER SEVEN

RHEIMS, JULY, 1429

JACQUES D'ARC and Durand Lassois had never, in their wildest dreams, imagined that they would ever attend a coronation. Even when tidings of the French victories had reached them, the notion of riding all the way to Rheims to see the Dauphin anointed and enthroned would never have occurred to them had not invitations arrived.

Not only Jacques and Lassois were bidden to attend, but four other invitations had come, to be distributed as Monsieur d'Arc thought fit. It had cost him a couple of sleepless nights, for his wife and three sons were eager to see Joan again; yet it was surely selfish to want to keep everything a family affair. And if all the d'Arcs went off to Rheims, who could be trusted to look after the farm and the sheep?

Then Jacquemin had announced that he intended to remain at home, so that Jean and Pierre could go; and Zabillet asked, smilingly, if anybody thought for an instant that a woman past forty could go careering around the countryside. That meant that one of the invitations could go to Jean Morel who had been one of Joan's godparents at her baptism, and the other to Geradin d'Epinal who had been so good about riding back and forth to Vaucouleurs to glean information about Joan's latest exploit.

There had even been a small escort of cavalry to guide the men northward to Rheims, and at Vaucouleurs they had been joined by de Metz and de Poulengy, who told them that the Maid was travelling slowly towards Rheims.

'She stopped on the way to take the submissions of Auxerre and Troyes!' de Metz said with a grin. 'And she has sent messengers to Rheims ordering the Archbishop to make ready for the Coronation.'

'The country bows down to her smallest whim!' de Poulengy exclaimed. 'It is the pucelle alone who has hurried on this coronation. Several of the captains felt she ought to take Paris before the ceremonies were arranged; and the Dauphin had been idling about at Loches and Gien, trying to decide what to do next. But Joan has spurred on the entire Court.'

'A remarkable girl!' exclaimed Jean Morel. 'I'm her godfather, you know. I held Joan in my arms on the day of her baptism and I said then, "This is a remarkable child!"'

'An angel from Heaven,' murmured de Metz.

Jacques d'Arc remained uneasily silent. It was difficult to reconcile the little girl whom he had sent out to watch the sheep with this remote goddess they were all talking about. He had not seen his daughter for seven months, ever since she had walked out of the house without saying anything, and stolen off to Vaucouleurs. At the time he'd wanted to drag her back, beat her soundly, and get her wed before she caused any more trouble. But Zabillet surprisingly, had put her foot down.

'Let the girl do what she has to do,' she had said. 'Let her have her chance.'

Zabillet was usually such a good, meek wife that Jacques had been dumbfounded to hear her express such an unconventional opinion. He'd been so astonished that he'd let the advice stand. Since then, there'd been nothing but reports of his daughter's progress.

But from Joan herself there had been no word and he wondered if she had grown proud and intended to keep him at a polite distance.

Even after they entered the gates of Rheims and had been lodged at a handsome inn in the Rue du Parvis, his mind was uneasy. The streets outside were bustling with people and it was a relief to seek the quietness of an inner room where an ample supper had been laid. But

Jacques was quite unable to do justice to the excellent meal. Several people had already whispered together and pointed him out and he was embarrassed, for the first time in his life, by his country manners.

The dishes were cleared away; the lamps were lit; de Metz and de Poulengy took their leave; but there was no sign of Joan. Then, just as Jacques was going to suggest they retire for the night, there was a babble of voices outside the door and Joan walked in.

For a second, Jacques wondered if his eyes were deceiving him. Was this tall, sunburnt girl with her hair shining blue-black really his daughter? She wore a tunic of fine golden stuff with deep fur cuffs on the trumpet shaped sleeves, and her hose were white satin. The three men with her were wrapped in velvet cloaks and their fingers glittered with jewels.

Then Joan came forward with her hands outstretched, and suddenly they were all talking at once, laughing and exclaiming and exchanging gossip. The three men with Joan were being presented, and Jacques was storing their names and appearances in his memory.

'The Duke of Alençon is extremely handsome with very gay, laughing eyes,' he would tell Zabillet later. 'Then there was de Vignolles whom they call La Hire, a real fighting man if ever I saw one. Oh, and there was Jean Dunois, the Governor of Orleans himself. A most likeable fellow, who asked after your health. Joan addresses him as 'Bastard', and only his closest friends are allowed to call him that.'

There would be much more to relate. How Joan had given him a bag full of gold coins as a present from the Dauphin; how she had declared that a special proclamation was to be drawn up, at her request, excusing Domremy and Greux from the payment of all taxes to the end of time; how she had given Jean Morel a bundle containing her old red dress which she had carried in her saddle-bag through all the campaigns; how she had told them she intended to buy a little house at Orleans so that she might have a place that was entirely her own in the city she had freed.

He would have to cheer his wife with such news because he was leaving Pierre and Jean with their sister. He had expected Jean to remain behind but Pierre was scarcely fifteen and Zabillet had spoilt him. But Joan had simply declared that she needed her brothers, and that was the end of the matter.

He would tell her, too, how Joan had had to visit him after dark because when she showed her face in public during the day she was mobbed by the adoring people. And he would describe the sword that Joan carried in battle.

'A magic sword, Zabillet! The blessed Saint Michael left it for her to find, but she must never strike a blow with it or its power will be broken. She showed me her banner, too, a white standard with the face of Our Lord and the world held up by two angels and *Jesu Maria* painted on it. And she has four horses and rides them in turn!'

It was all so strange and splendid, and there were some things impossible to describe.

Jacques knew he would never find words for the Coronation ceremony itself.

To begin with, there was the huge cathedral into which the village church would have fitted a hundred times with room to spare. Nobody from Domremy had ever seen such magnificent stained glass, such a profusion of lilies spilling over the gold and silver of the altar and banked up in great heaps around the walls. There were red carpets laid down the aisles, and musicians in silver tunics stood in groups and sang.

As for the people! Jacques had felt uncommonly smart in his orange doublet and grey hose that had been bought at Taul and cost as much as half a cow; but he paled into insignificance beside the Dukes and princes in their crimson and white, and the bishops in gold and silver. And the women with their white faces, and pointed head-dresses, and silken dresses of blue, lemon, green and pink, with crystals sparkling round their necks and pendants of amethyst and aquamarine dipping into the valleys of their breasts above their low-cut bodices—on second thoughts, he would say very little about the women.

The Dauphin—only one must remember to call him King Charles now, of course—had looked and behaved most regally. He was rather smaller than Jacques had expected, but every inch a monarch. And throughout the proceedings Joan had stood by his side. She had worn a suit of armour, gilded silver, and a red cloak embroidered with green nettles had floated from her shoulders for these were the heraldic badges of Orleans. Her head was bare, and she had carried her sword and her standard.

All his life, Jacques would remember how his daughter's face had glowed when the great doors were opened, and a man in full armour on an armoured horse had ridden up the aisle, to present the golden ampoulla to the Archbishop. The man was Gilles de Raiz, Marshal of France, and the ampoulla contained the holy oil brought down to earth by the Holy Ghost at the baptism of King Clovis generations before.

No man might call himself King of France until he had been anointed with the sacred oil. Looking at his daughter, Jacques guessed the thoughts passing through her mind. The war might not be over, but Charles was King. and nothing could go wrong.

SOISSONS, AUGUST, 1429

'Is it safe to talk to you, Majesty?'

La Tremouille hesitated on the threshold, looking, thought Charles, rather like an agitated duck.

'Perfectly safe. I gave orders that we were to be left alone.'

'And the Maid?'

'She has gone to the tilting yard with d'Alençon.'

'It is difficult to see Your Majesty alone these days,' La Tremouille remarked, closing the door and coming to kneel before the high-backed chair where the King was lounging.

'I give constant audiences,' Charles yawned.

'To d'Alençon, and to Dunois, and to the Pucelle. Where she is, they go! And she is always with Your Majesty. Sometimes I fear you forget old friends.'

'Have I any old friends?'

'More than Your Majesty knows. And we worry, Sire, because we can see the dangers you are running.'

'What danger?' Charles sat up and waved the Duke to a stool.

'Sire, it is not for a humble subject to remind you, but six months ago you faced ruin. Your armies were beaten, your treasury empty, your very title called in question.'

'Until Joan came.'

'Exactly!' La Tremouille nodded and placed his thick palms together. 'The Maid came and you, sensing in her the power of God decided to use her.'

'She hasn't been unsuccessful.'

'On the contrary! The list of her triumphs grows longer and longer. The whole country is at her feet, and she is well aware of it. She dresses magnificently and rides through the streets, displaying herself to the crowds.'

'She's very young,' Charles said.

'Is she? Sometimes, when she looks at me with those odd blue eyes, I wonder if she isn't older than any of us. You know, as Your Majesty was being crowned, I stole a glance at the Maid's face. Do you know what was written upon it? Envy! Envy, Sire, of you and your position.'

'Oh, surely not!' the King protested.

'I don't think she was even aware of her own feelings. She is, as you say, very young, too young to be aware of her own power or the extent of her ambition. You began by using her, but she may end by trying to use you.'

'I trust the Maid,' Charles said, obstinately.

'In your position you cannot afford to trust anybody,' La Tremouille said, earnestly. 'Tell me what advice the Maid has given you recently.'

'She wants to sweep on towards Paris and Campiegne,' Charles said. 'She urges me to unite the entire country.'

He broke off, staring at La Tremouille who had flung up his hands.

'It is as I feared, Majesty. In her lust for conquest, Joan will lose your throne for you. Or else so seriously weaken your position that you will rule, according to her pleasure. There is little chance for a further victory. You must know there is no more money to pay the army. The expenses of your Coronation—'

'The army will follow the Maid without payment.'

'Exactly! They will follow Joan but they will not stir a step for their lawful King. Even if there are more victories, if Paris falls, do you imagine the people will shout for you? They will shout for the Maid, as they shouted for her at Orleans.'

'Then what am I to do?'

'Be subtle, Sire. Let your people see that you are a true King, not a weakling propped up on his throne by a woman. Soon, the glory that surrounds Joan will fade. Oh, she has brought victory, but what does victory mean to a woman whose husband has fallen in battle, or a farmer whose crops have been ruined by military wagons? Think how eagerly the people would shout for you if you concluded a just and honourable peace.'

'With the English? Joan would never allow it!'

La Tremouille rose with dignity, wrapping his robe around him.

'I see that I must, in future, seek audience with the Pucelle, since it is she, and not King Charles VII, who reigns in France,' he said, loftily.

'Wait a minute! Wait. Sit down again.'

The King had also risen and was plucking eagerly at his courtier's sleeve.

'To hear you tell me what the Maid intends to do? I can hear that from her own lips if I follow her to the tiltyard where all your other so-called friends have gone!'

'But what would you have me do? How can I make peace? Who would listen?'

La Tremouille sat down and began to talk, soothingly and respectfully.

It sounded beautifully simple, Charles thought. The Duke of Burgundy was willing to surrender Paris if the King would show good faith by signing a fifteen day truce.

'Why should the Duke of Burgundy be willing to do that?' he asked, doubtfully.

'How can one fathom the intentions of a Burgundian?' La Tremouille returned. 'It's my belief that he has been disillusioned by his English allies, and I know him to be short of money. He sent his envoy to me in the first place because—'

He hesitated.

'Because what?'

'Sire, forgive me! But it is generally said that every message which comes to the King must first be approved by the Pucelle. Burgundy knows me to be completely loyal to your interests, and so sent his envoy to me.'

Charles moved to the window and stood looking out. He could see a group of courtiers riding across the bridge. In the midst of them, a boyish figure in a tunic of chain mail was laughing. Her head was flung back and the sun sparkled on the diamond collar round her throat. The King remembered the soberly clad girl who had recognized him at Chinon five months before.

When he turned round again, his weak face was resentful.

'I'll sign this treaty privately,' he said. 'If you will make the necessary arrangements, we can still conclude this peace.'

'And you will never regret it, Sire!'

As La Tremouille went towards his own quarters, Joan

clattered up the staircase with d'Alençon and Dunois on her heels.

She made an eloquent face in the direction of the Duke's retreating back.

'What mischief has old sowface been hatching, I wonder!'

'Perhaps he has been adding up his accounts,' d'Alençon suggested, and there was a shout of laughter for La Tremouille's stinginess was well known.

'As long as he has not been talking to the King,' Joan muttered, and a frown creased her brows.

'You don't trust La Tremouille, do you?'

'Do *you*?' she retorted to Dunois.

'None of us do. But there is no proof of his treachery.'

'No proof except the smell of evil and a shiver down my back whenever he looks at me.'

'Have your voices warned you against him?'

Joan shook her head, forbearing to add that her voices had grown fainter since the Coronation. She no longer heard them clearly amid the gossip of the Court.

Three days later, she stood, weeping, before the King, while the nobles clustered behind her, dismayed and shaken.

'This is treachery!' Joan sobbed. 'We should have marched on Paris immediately after the coronation. I held back because you would not have it so. I held back and you have made peace with the Burgundians. You make a shameful treaty just as I bring you a new ally.'

'What ally?'

'You remember, Sire, how before I rode to Chinon, I went to Nancy to see the Duke of Lorraine. I asked then if he would allow Rene d'Anjou to join us. I told you about it, Sire! We received news this morning that the Duc d'Anjou is on his way here, to swear fealty to you.'

'How is it that such information was given first to you?' La Tremouille asked. 'And why did you not inform His Majesty at once?'

'It was to be a surprise,' Joan said, and her lip trembled childishly.

'A surprise! An important duke comes over to our side and you keep it as a surprise! Did it not occur to you that His Majesty might wish to arrange a fitting reception for so important a personage? Or were you afraid lest d'Anjou be given more honour than you?'

'He's right, you know,' Charles nodded gravely.

'I'm sorry if I behaved wrongly, Sire, but all this has nothing to do with the treaty. We must capture Paris. Can't you see that? Can't you understand that treaties are made only to be broken, that they merely cause delays?'

But the King turned away, whispering to La Tremouille. Joan's eyes overflowed again and her brothers moved to stand protectively on each side of her.

'You're tired,' Charles said. 'You're tired and over-wrought, and begin to imagine me ungrateful. Why don't you go to Orleans for a while? Buy that house you were talking about, or take a little trip back to your village.'

It was useless. When her visions were strong and clear, she could sway whole armies. But now her visions were faint and their words were cloudy, and when she tried to make people understand, her eloquence drained away. She was aware of only one thing, something her voices had told her many times.

She flung it at the King now.

'Sire, don't waste me! Use me well, for I will last only a year!'

But Charles was whispering to La Tremouille again, and wasn't even listening.

PARIS, SEPTEMBER, 1429

Minguet was afraid. He expected to be afraid before a battle until the excitement and the shouting drove away his terror; but this was different, for now, in the midst of the fighting his mouth was still dry and his heart thumped painfully.

Yet everything seemed as it always was. Joan rode her black horse, with her standard in her hand, and Minguet was near enough to hear her clear voice urging on the men.

The soldiers themselves followed her readily as they always did, but too many of them were falling wounded. The enemy were not acting as they had acted in previous battles. They were not, Minguet saw, running away. Instead they were retaliating, and although the Pucelle's men flung themselves time and time again back into the struggle, the gates of Paris held firm.

Minguet, backing his horse out of cannon-range tried to puzzle out the reason why everything was going wrong, but it was difficult to think clearly amid the confusion.

In his own mind, it had begun with the signing of the truce between the King and the Duke of Burgundy. Everybody knew now that Burgundy had used the delay in order to send urgent messages to the Duke of Bedford for English reinforcements, so that instead of surrendering Paris to the King at the end of fifteen days, the Duke had declared his intention of holding it for the King of England.

Even then, the King had tried to make another treaty, and had refused to dismiss La Tremouille although it was an open secret that the fat duke was taking bribes from all sides.

Had Minguet been in Joan's shoes, he would have left court and sulked at home until they were forced to ask his help again. But Joan went on begging the King to make war, and meanwhile the towns of Beauvais and Compiegne made submission to the French.

The surrender of Beauvais had cheered Joan up immensely. She had been very anxious to get her hands on to its bishop, who had supported the English ever since the Treaty of Troyes and was known to have waxed rich on his treachery; but when the French marched into the town,

Pierre Cauchon had fled. He was now in Rouen which was still in the English grasp, and Joan had already declared she intended to take Rouen and put the bishop on trial there.

Meanwhile, there remained Paris, and Minguet would never forget how bitterly the Maid had wept as she stood on the hill at St Denis, and looked over the surrounding countryside to the spires of the capital.

'If the blessed Saint Genevieve could see her city in the hands of foreigners, she, too, would weep!' Joan had cried. 'When Attila the Hun was almost at the gates of Paris, her prayers turned him aside. But she was a great saint and her words were more powerful than armies. Yet surely she could not have loved this land more than I do!'

So now they were attacking the walls of that proud city where Burgundians and English stalked the streets where once Charlemagne and Clovis had walked in triumphant procession.

'God sleeps!' the Duke of Alençon cried, appearing suddenly at Minguet's side. 'The Pucelle is carried from the field with an arrow in her thigh, and our men are falling back on all sides. This is a sad defeat!'

'Is the Maid badly hurt?'

'I think not, but we cannot make any progress if she is not here. Go to her, boy, lest she has need of your services.'

D'Alençon galloped away and the trumpets sounded the official retreat.

As usual the Maid's lodging was crammed with her followers, most of whom were making no attempt to disguise their disappointment. Joan was behaving, they considered, in a manner quite unlike herself. Her wound was not serious but she was acting as if it were almost a mortal hurt. She had fainted when they pulled out the arrow, and when the physicians had recommended cauterization she had screamed out that nobody was to burn her, for above all things she dreaded the pain of fire. She had been bled and bandaged, instead, and was grumbling that the dressing was too tight and the room too crowded.

'Everywhere I go, there are people to trouble me and harass me. I cannot even be sick in peace but you must all burst in upon my privacy. And who sounded the order for retreat? If it was you, Bastard, I swear I'll have your head! How is it that you all have to be babied into battle? Was it any reason to stop fighting because I had an arrow in my leg! Must I be taxed beyond my strength and provide you with courage from my own small stock, because you have none of your own!'

They drifted out sheepishly while she fretted and complained, and sent Minguet for wine and then declared it was sour, and boxed the physician's ears for having suggested she was feverish, and then broke into another passion of tears, declaring that between them all they would kill her.

And this time she did not recover her spirits. Her wound healed and the army offered thanks for her recovery, but she stayed in her lodgings, staring up at the ceiling for hours, threatening to execute Dunois two or three times a day, and forever weeping bitterly.

When the order to abandon Paris and disband her troops came from the King, Minguet expected an explosion of temper, but the Maid listened as Dunois contemptuously read the royal proclamation and said nothing at all. She did not even order her troops to be drawn up for a passing out inspection, but told d'Alençon that she wished to ride quietly to Saint Denis for there was one more task to be done.

The Duke was alarmed, so alarmed that he sent a hasty letter to his wife delaying once again his return home, and rode after Joan, leaving Dunois and d'Aulun to deal with such matters as the payment of the soldiers and the treatment of the wounded. Behind him, the closed gates of Paris mocked at him.

The Maid's usual lodging was deserted, save for Minguet

who sat disconsolately on the doorstep and raised a woe-begone, freckled face.

'She has gone to the Cathedral, my lord Duke,' he said, in reply to the other's query. 'She said that if you came she wished you to join her there.'

The Cathedral was empty as the Duke strode in, and his feet echoed on the stone floor. A monk in black vestments glided silently past and went towards the crypts, with no more than a brief glance at the courtier.

The main altar glittered, cold and magnificent, it's sanctuary lamp glowing redly. D'Alençon knelt automatically, and as he rose, saw Joan coming towards him from a side altar where a statue of the Virgin smiled down benignly.

The Maid was in a page's suit of white satin and looked pale and tired.

'You should not walk the streets alone,' he began scoldingly, in a whisper. 'Did you come here to pray? Minguet said you wished to see me.'

He broke off, following her pointing finger and seeing the gilded armour piled up at the foot of the Virgin's statue.

'I have renounced it,' she said, quietly. 'My armour lies here as an offering to God.'

'Then you're giving up?' He stared at her incredulously.

'I cannot fight the English and the Burgundians if my anointed King prefers to make treaties with them.'

'But the King is wrong! We know the King is wrong. You must save his throne for him in spite of himself!'

He had raised his voice slightly and she put her finger to her lips and led him to a corner seat, where she established herself beside him.

'You don't understand, my friend. It is not because my King listens to the evil counsel of La Tremouille that I must cease to fight. I will take up arms once more, when I hear my voices again.'

'But surely you still hear them?'

'Not clearly,' she said, sadly. 'For weeks my voices have

not spoken clearly, and my saints have not visited me. Before I came to Court I heard them often and at that time there was little hope of my ever attempting to do what I have done. Now, when I need them more than ever, they mumble and mutter in my brain. They did not instruct me to attack Paris, you know. That was something I tried to do all by myself, and I failed.'

'We will take Paris yet!'

'Of course, but I dare not try again until I receive definite instructions. By myself, without the guidance of the holy ones, I can do nothing except lead men to death. I have no power in myself. Dunois knows it and is returning to Court. So are La Hire, de Raiz and d'Aulun.'

Impulsively, d'Alençon seized her hands, holding them closely against him.

'If you ordered me at this moment, Pucelle, to march to the gates of Paris and attack, I would do so, if you were with me. The Bastard will, in the end, obey the King for they have been companions since childhood. De Raiz thinks of his titles and his fine estates, but I will follow you wherever you choose to go. I believe in you, Joan, not in voices I can't hear and angels I never see.'

'You will tempt me to the sin of pride yet,' she said, with a laugh that was half a sob.

'Not pride, Joan. And even if it were, haven't you the right to be a little proud of your achievements? You have done what no other woman has ever done. You have ridden into battle, inspired men to deeds of great valour, conquered the enemy time and time again. If it were not for you, Charles would have neither crown nor Kingdom. We should all be obedient to you.'

'But I also must be obedient,' Joan said quickly. 'I must obey God who sends me his wishes by Saint Michael, and after God I must obey the King.'

'And if their wishes conflict?' the Duke asked dryly.

'Then I will obey God if he speaks clearly to me,' she said simply, 'but if my voices are silent I must do the

King's will. I will not attack Paris again on my own account.'

'So you will submit to being Court favourite.' D'Alençon got up and walked away, disappointment stabbing him.

'Life at Court can be gay and pleasant,' she exclaimed. 'I will have to spend the rest of my life milking cows and watching sheep when my task is completed. Don't grudge me a soft bed and a leg of chicken now!'

'Pucelle, I grudge you nothing. I only beg you not to lose heart. Even if your voices never return, you must go on! You said once that you would not last a year. At the end of that time, your public life will be over, and you must have completed your work by then. The whole army will follow you. I said I would obey you.'

'Come and sit down again!' Joan begged. 'And stop shouting, or the whole of Saint Denis will imagine there is a riot in the Cathedral! Now, listen to me. You said that you would obey me—'

'To the death!'

'But I don't want your death. I promised your wife that I would send you home safely, and that is what I intend to do. I want you to go back to your estates in Beaumont.'

'To leave you and go home!'

'Is this the man who would not amuse himself in camp with wine and song, because he had not written to his wife that day? I want you to leave me, d'Alençon. When my campaign begins again, I'll send for you. I promise it.'

'Then you do value me!' he said, lightly, to conceal his hurt.

Joan hesitated a moment, then met his eyes frankly, while into her voice crept a note he had never heard before.

'Dear d'Alençon, my life has not been the kind of life God intends for most women. I think I always sensed that, and so refused to make a marriage. But if I could have felt desire, as other women do, it would have been for a man like you. Hold that in your heart. Dunois is my friend; so are de Raiz, Saint Severe, and d'Aulun, but of all my captains, you are the one I have loved above all others.'

Then she flung her arms around his neck, kissed him on both cheeks, and went to kneel again before the altar where her armour was piled up. When d'Alençon left the church, she never turned her head.

BOURGES, OCTOBER, 1429

'If we had the money, Sire, we could wage war with impunity,' La Tremouille was saying.

'More taxes?' the King suggested.

'My liege, if it were possible to raise more money in such a way, then we would have done so. But the treasury is utterly exhausted! We must keep both England and Burgundy quiet by extending the truce. The Archbishop agrees with me.'

'Indeed I do, Your Majesty,' bowed de Chartres.

'The pucelle wishes to leave Court,' the King said, apparently changing the subject.

'I thought she seemed more content since the withdrawal from Paris,' the Duke frowned.

'She has asked me for permission to join d'Alençon at Beaumont. His wife has sent an invitation to her—what are you shaking your head over, de Chartres?'

'I dislike the notion of a young unmarried girl being so intimate with a married man.'

'Oh, fiddlesticks! Joan has spent months sleeping alongside married men when she was waging war. Why should she not spend a holiday with one of them now, especially as his wife will be there?'

The Archbishop and the Duke exchanged glances, then La Tremouille leaned forward, with his hands on his knees and candour written all over his face.

'It is not the moral aspect that concerns me, so much as the political aspect,' he said, frankly. 'If Joan wishes to leave Court and join d'Alençon, then she is not as content as I had supposed, and in my view, a discontented courtier ought to remain where her actions can be supervised, shall we say?'

'You think Joan intends to plot against me with d'Alençon? Why I trust them as much as I trust myself.'

'Your Majesty's feelings do you credit,' the Archbishop said, 'but you must realize, Sire, that your experience of the full depravity of human beings has been limited.'

'When my own mother declared my titles to be unlawful, I began to realize such depravity existed,' Charles snapped.

'Then you are already aware of the depths to which a woman will sink,' de Chartres said smoothly. 'I like not this sudden restlessness, nor this craving for d'Alençon's company. I like it not!'

'Then what can I do?'

As the King asked the usual despairing question, his Councillors relaxed.

'If I were in your position, Sire, I would send d'Alençon into Normandy. There are riots there to be quelled. And I would give the pucelle some work to do. Order her to assemble the troops together and attack one of the smaller towns along the Loire. Shall we say St Pierre-le-Moutier? And if she is successful there, we can send her to La Charite? To besiege those towns won't contravene our existing treaty, and it will give the girl something to do.'

'And d'Alençon must go to Normandy?'

'Oh, most definitely, Sire. It would be most unwise to allow the two of them to come together for a while.'

'May I say, Your Majesty, how much we applaud your decision? It shows both wisdom and strength,' La Tremouille interposed.

'And if Joan won't go to St Pierre-le-Moutier?'

'But you are her anointed King, Sire!' cried de Chartres. 'Under God, we must all obey you.'

'And you were not, of course, going to send Joan in her unofficial capacity. You would, of course, give her a military title. A commander of the army, at least!'

'And as a commander of the French army, she would be bound to obey her military superiors.'

Charles felt dizzy as their soft voices beat on. They sat on each side of him, and their breath was sour.

When they were not present, he was able to ask himself if the rumours were true. Were the Duke and the Archbishop really taking English bribes? He knew they hated the pucelle, but was there anything more in their hatred than personal spite? Did Joan really hope to set herself up as a rival power, with d'Alençon to support her? D'Alençon was so gay and generous, but could he also be untrustworthy?

The King's head ached with unaccustomed thinking. He longed to bring the interview to an end and seek solace in Agnes's arms. Only in his mistress's bed and sometimes in his wife's, did he feel himself to be the all-conquering King he had tried to become.

His Councillors were begging to be excused, assuring him they would draw up the necessary proclamations for his signature. He couldn't recall what decisions he had made, but no doubt he would remember. Meanwhile, he needed a tisane to soothe his headache and perhaps some music to carry his thoughts to a pleasanter sphere.

Outside the door, La Tremouille and the Archbishop of Rheims looked at each other in concern.

'The King still favours the Maid,' the Duke said, uneasily. 'He is grateful to her for the success she has brought him.'

'But not so grateful that he will allow her to rule France,' murmured de Chartres.

The two men nodded in complete accord, for they had no intention of allowing anybody to be the power behind the throne except themselves.

'If the Maid wins more victories, may it not further tip the scales in her favour?' de Chartres asked.

'She will not take La Charite,' La Tremouille said, smiling into his beard. 'The English are well-entrenched there, and our own troops are very short of weapons. And, naturally, with the exchequer so grossly depleted, we could not at the present time undertake to spend more money.'

The Archbishop bowed gravely and they separated. La Tremouille returned to his own lodging to write a note in cipher to the Duke of Bedford, and de Chartres repaired to his private chapel, to pray for sinners.

CHAPTER EIGHT

JARGEAU, NOVEMBER, 1429

'DEAR heavens! Not another miracle worker!'

Joan stared at her hostess in dismay.

'A most impressive one,' Marguerite La Touroulde assured her. 'Her name is Catherine La Rochelle and she comes with the personal recommendation of Brother Richard himself.'

'That is no recommendation at all!' Joan said, crisply. 'I met Brother Richard at Troyes, and he was a complete fool!'

'Why, he is one of the most fiery preachers in the country!' Marguerite said. 'He spends all his time calling on people to repent, for he fears the end of the world is at hand.'

'He's a loud-mouthed fanatic,' Joan said, with distaste. 'When he came to meet me he was hung about with amulets and stinking of incense. He said he had protected himself lest I cast the evil eye on him. Who is this Catherine La Rochelle anyway? Not another Pierronne, I hope!'

Although she was slightly shocked at Joan's disrespectful tone, Marguerite could not help laughing.

Less than a week before, some half-crazed girl, calling herself La Pierronne, had arrived at the treasurer's house and asked to see Joan. She had then thrown herself on the ground, writhing and foaming at the mouth and crying out that she could see angels.

'Poor creature!' Joan said. 'We ought not to mock her, for she meant no harm. She told me that God comes down to talk to her regularly, wearing a red tunic and a long white robe. But she is sick in her mind and ought to be treated gently.'

'This Catherine is still waiting,' hinted Marguerite. 'She

has been travelling for two days and has found no lodging yet, so I offered to let her stay here. Perhaps I should have consulted you first.'

'My dear Marguerite, this is your house! You may invite whom you like to stay,' Joan exclaimed.

'And you will see her?'

'To please you,' Joan smiled.

She watched the older woman with affection as she bustled from the room. Marguerite La Touroulde was a little bird-like being who ceaselessly twittered around her important guest. Joan liked her immensely, for Marguerite, despite her wealth and fine clothes, was not too grand to sit and spin or take a hand with the baking. She had no children of her own, and Joan shrewdly suspected that the lack of them caused her to keep busier than she need have been.

Her heart sank when the newcomer was ushered into the room, for Catherine La Rochelle was draped in white wool and festooned with an ornate crucifix.

'Blessings upon you, Pucelle! I greet my spiritual sister!'

Catherine flung out her arms in an expansive gesture, and Joan hastily reached for her tapestry frame, remarking, with as much cordiality as she could muster, that she liked to keep busy.

'Oh! Are you *sewing*?' Catherine sat down opposite Joan and regarded the younger girl with awe. 'How frightfully clever of you! I have been so much occupied with spiritual matters that I never learned anything practical. My visions take up so much of my time that I need to save my strength for them.'

'I'm making some cushion covers as a gift for Madame La Touroulde.'

'Cushion covers! How quaint! Joan of the Lilies sewing cushion covers!'

'I don't spend all my time sitting on a horse, you know,' Joan said, mildly.

Marguerite was offering cakes and wine but Catherine

had turned away with a little shriek.

'Oh, no cake! I absolutely adore those little sugar things, but they're so bad for the soul! And only a drop of wine. The teeniest, weeniest drop! One doesn't wish to cloud the aura, does one?'

'Cloud the what?' Joan asked.

'The aura, dear. The light of the spirit. Mine is silver, you know. That's because I'm so closely in contact with the other world. Yours is probably silver too.'

'Is it indeed?' Joan laid her work aside and bit into a sugar cake.

'But don't you *know*? Haven't your angels told you? My white lady told me all about it. She appears to me every night and we have fantastically interesting conversations. She told me that I have the power of discovering buried treasure. If I stand upon soil where gold is buried, my feet vibrate.'

'How unpleasant for you!'

'Ah! when one is gifted, one must expect some personal discomfort. I have the gift of tongues too, which is really why I came. If you would like me to mediate for the King with the Duke of Burgundy, I assure you I could positively *stun* him with words!'

'The Duke of Burgundy,' Joan said fiercely, 'needs to be stunned with a battle-axe.'

'You're so warlike!' Catherine trilled. 'I do so want my white lady to meet you.'

'*I'd* rather enjoy meeting your white lady,' Joan said, dryly.

'Tonight!' Catherine sprang up. 'You must watch with me tonight. Oh, do say you'll watch with me.'

Joan consented, and the other broke into a flutter of excitement.

Never, thought Joan could the prospect of a vision have created so much fuss and bother! Catherine La Rochelle must have a room far away from the main quarters of the house and the room must be draped in black and swept

142

clean of all rushes. There must be no furniture except a small table and two high-backed chairs, and the fire must be of pine logs and pitch.

'I'm sure she's a very spiritual person,' whispered Marguerite, 'but I do wish she wouldn't order my servants about quite so loudly. They are really not used to it!'

When darkness fell and the doors were closed behind them, Joan expected her companion to pray quietly until the vision came. But Catherine La Rochelle had evidently no taste for silence. She settled herself in the most comfortable of the two chairs and proceeded to give Joan a year by year account of her life, beginning when, as a child, her parents had seen an archangel floating over her cradle.

Catherine had, thought Joan, the most boring voice she had ever heard, and the most long-winded method of telling a story. Her voice went on and on in its interminable recital, and Joan's eyelids began to droop long before the hour of midnight.

Joan awoke to a room filled with daylight and to Catherine La Rochelle's voice, which had apparently never stopped.

'The spirit was willing, but the flesh was weak, my dear. I tried so hard to wake you up, but the white lady could only stay a few minutes. Never mind, we must not be too disappointed. She will come again tonight, I'm sure.'

'Then we'll try again tonight.'

Catherine La Rochelle missed the deceptive innocence in the Maid's voice, and quite failed to see the mischief in her blue eyes.

Marguerite La Touroulde really exerted herself that day to entertain her guest.

When Mass had been said, she took the young woman on a protracted shopping trip, and after dinner they visited the public baths. Joan did not appear until after supper, when she arrived in the black-draped room looking vigorous and bright-eyed.

'You'll be anxious for an introduction to the King, no doubt?' she began, when they were both seated by the fire.

'Oh, if it could be arranged! Little unimportant me! to be presented at Court!' Catherine raised her eyes and hands in an affected manner that made Joan want to slap her.

The night wore on slowly. Catherine was evidently in no mood to talk. Indeed, more than once her head drooped and something suspiciously like a snore escaped her. Joan, on the other hand, was feeling the benefit of a day spent mainly in sleep. With lively pleasure, she launched into an exquisitely tedious, high flown account of her own life, frequently interrupting her narrative to shake Catherine awake and ask her if the white lady would appear soon.

'Soon! Very soon!'

Catherine blinked sleepily at Joan, who immediately pulled her to her feet, demanding a brisk turn about the room and asking yet again when the vision would arrive.

When dawn streaked the sky, the Maid emerged, calling cheerfully for her horse so that she could go to Mass.

'The white lady didn't come,' she said loudly to Marguerite, 'but no matter! We'll stay awake again tonight and the night after, until she does arrive.'

Behind her, Catherine La Rochelle, red-eyed and miserable, sagged limply against the wall.

'I'll be back in an hour, and we'll do a little sightseeing before we begin the second watch,' Joan continued relentlessly.

As she swung her leg over her horse, she grinned happily. Something told her that by the time she returned from church Catherine La Rochelle would have fled.

DOMREMY, DECEMBER, 1429

Jacques d'Arc did not believe that it was possible to be a happier man. Neither did he consider it necessary to hide his feelings. When he came out of his small house with its smart new coat of whitewash, and looked across the road where the stream glittered under its thin covering of ice, one might have noticed, immediately, his air of well-being. His beard was freshly trimmed and even the feather in his cap had a perky air.

He leaned nonchalantly against the wall, listening to the bells pealing from the tower of the rebuilt church.

'Seigneur Jacques du Lys,' he murmured, rolling the words around his tongue as if they were sugar-plums.

Jacques d'Arc, farmer, was now Knight of the Lilies. And his wife could style herself as Lady, and Jacquemin, Jean and Pierre could also put 'Knight' before their names. And Joan might call herself 'Princess', which was the grandest of all.

The imposing document tied with red and green ribbons and stamped with the great seal of King Charles VII had been brought to Domremy, and read aloud in the church and in the market square. Now, carefully stretched over a wooden frame and protected by a sheet of glass, bought at great expense in Vaucouleurs, the royal proclamation dangled proudly from a nail in the main living-room.

'A wonderful Christmas present,' Jacques said aloud. 'Did you know, wife, that Joan asked the King to delay our ennoblement until the season of the Nativity? She wanted it to be a surprise for us.'

Zabillet, who had come out to stand beside her husband, nodded, smiling.

'And she has bought a house for you at Orleans,' marvelled Jacques. 'Sir Robert said she intended to buy it for herself, but at the last moment she asked for it to be bought in your name. And did you see the doublet she sent to Jacquemin? All gold and silver threadwork, and even the sleeves lined with ermine! And the food-parcels! One for every house in the village. Rabbits, capons, pheasants and Rhenish wine; and the Lord knows what else!'

'We are indeed fortunate in our child,' Zabillet agreed.

Not for worlds would she have admitted that not all the

gifts in creation could make up for the fact that Joan was spending Christmas at Orleans. She had hoped so hard that Joan would come back home for a little while. She had even cleaned out her daughter's old room and arranged some dried leaves and berries in a copper vase. But Joan had sent word that she would not return to Domremy until her mission was completed. And Jean and Pierre had elected to remain with their sister.

There was only Jacquemin to share their Christmas goose, and Jacquemin was not well. He said nothing as he went quietly about his work on the farm, but Zabillet heard him coughing at night. He had seemed pleased with his fine new doublet but she guessed he would have been more pleased if Jean or Pierre had come home to help with the lambing. They were both captains now and enjoying Court life immensely, but she would have liked them all to have sat down to their Christmas dinner together.

'I thought we would have the coat of arms put over the front door,' Jacques mused. 'We have the right to bear the lilies of France now, and a sword on a blue background. Joan chose the design herself, and I think it sounds very tasteful indeed.'

'Won't it be a little ostentatious?'

Jacques turned and stared at his wife. 'Upon my soul, Zabillet,' he said, at last. 'I simply don't understand you. Is there any other family in Domremy with the right to bear a coat of arms?'

'But everybody in Domremy already knows we have been ennobled,' she objected.

'And what of the visitors who will come here?' he demanded. 'All the fine lords and ladies will want to visit the house where the Maid was born. Heaven be praised that the Burgundians left our home standing! We must keep the place spick and span, for who knows? When Joan comes home, she may bring His Majesty with her.'

'No doubt you're right. I wish Joan would come soon though.'

'You can't expect her to throw up everything and rush back to the village!' Jacques argued. 'Now that she has taken St Pierre-le-Moutier she must press on!'

'But she didn't take La Charite.'

'Which is all the more reason for her to renew the attack,' her husband retorted.

'I'm sure you're right, dear. I don't understand these military matters,' Zabillet admitted meekly. 'Will you come in for some dinner now?'

'I thought I'd stroll over to wish Lebuin the compliments of the season,' Jacques said.

'Then I'll hold back the meal. But you'd better put on your cloak.'

'I'll put on the green one I bought for the Coronation. It's very warm.'

'And very bright! Cheerful, I mean,' she amended, hastily.

A few minutes later, she watched him striding grandly down the road, a conspicuous figure in emerald cloth.

She was glad the unpleasantness with Lebuin was over. Michel was still unmarried, and Zabillet wondered, sometimes, if he hoped, as she did, that one day Joan would come home again, prepared to lead a normal life. But perhaps they would expect Joan to marry a lord now.

Zabillet sighed, pulled her wrap more closely around herself, and went indoors. The fire was burning brightly in the central hearth, and the pans and kettles shone in rows along the wall. She took down one of the pans and began to slice beans into it, in readiness for their meal. When the dinner was prepared, she would put on her new blue dress and the little pearl ear-rings Jacques had brought her from Rheims.

On the wall opposite, the Act of Ennoblement splashed its colours. Zabillet looked up at the words she couldn't read, and began to cry, without understanding why she did so.

'You have the loveliest hair in the world, my sweet!'

Bertha let the words of her lover slide over her while his hands caressed her naked breasts and thighs. She had long forgotten her dreams of being loved by a decent young man. Many of the soldiers in the camp were decent enough, she supposed, but none of them loved her. It was ten years since she had followed the Englishman from Troyes, and there were times when she tried to remember his face. But many faces had passed before her eyes, and many bodies had laid beside her. Goddams and Frenchmen and Burgundians—take off their clothes and there was nothing to choose between them, she thought cynically.

Two of them had left her pregnant, but a wise-woman had given her physic to take upon the first occasion, and she had miscarried. The second child she had carried to its full time, and borne it in a ditch on the road to Paris. It had been a girl, and she had stifled it before it could cry and buried it in the soft earth scooped out by her hands. That was five years ago and she could not recall where the grave had been situated.

She squealed as the soldier's hand crept between her legs and the man hushed her fiercely.

'Don't make a noise! If you make a noise we will be discovered!'

'Who cares!'

She rolled away from him, staring through the tent flap at the starlit sky.

'We are not supposed to bring harlots into camp,' the man whispered.

'Why, whoever heard of an army without them!'

'It is the *pucelle's* order.'

'Oh, the *pucelle*!' Bertha spat and rolled over on to her back again. 'All I ever hear is that crazy woman's name! Is she so greedy she wants to sleep with every soldier in the army then?'

'She is the pucelle!' he said, shocked.

'Hah! and I bet your fine officers could tell you a thing or two about the pucelle! I'll reckon she's as big a whore as the rest of us, if the truth be known.'

'That's Burgundian talk,' he said, angrily.

'And sometimes the Burgundians talk good sense,' she retorted. 'Anyway, even if she is a virgin, that's no reason to make everybody else take a vow of chastity. And you don't all obey her. You don't imagine I'm the only harlot in the camp tonight, do you?'

'Just the noisiest one,' he said, and bent over her again.

When he finally slept, Bertha wriggled away and pulled on her dress. She was rather fond of that particular garment for a goddam with gentle hands had given her the money for it. That had been at Beauvais where she had gone after the fall of Patay. The soldier had been very young and so innocent she had had to show him what to do, but obviously he had appreciated the lesson because he had given her ten gold pieces. She corrected her wandering thoughts. The goddam had actually given her four gold pieces and she had stolen the rest from his doublet while he was struggling back into his hose.

She wondered idly if he had made good use of his instruction. She had never seen him since but had joined the Burgundians for a while, until one of them swore he'd slice up her face, for giving him the pox, and then she'd fled again.

She finished dressing and sat combing her hair, listening to the hooting of the owls in the forest as the stars paled and the sky grew lighter. Occasionally, a man called out restlessly in his sleep, and once she heard a smothered giggle.

She wondered if this small force would take the town of Melun which lay to the south. The English were still at Paris, but they were ringed round by towns that had made submission to the French. Sometimes, she wished she could care which side won, and sometimes she knew that it really didn't matter.

When her hair lay thick and smooth over her shoulders, she lay down and went to sleep without dreaming.

She awoke to the shouting of men, the jangling of harness, and the neighing of horses. Her soldier was already pulling on the padded leather breastplate and iron helmet that would protect him from enemy arrows.

'You slept well,' he remarked.

'A clear conscience!' She yawned and sat up, hugging her knees.

'Well, you'd better be off. I have to pull down the tent and return it.'

'Isn't it yours?'

'Did you ever meet a common soldier with a tent all to himself? I borrowed it from a Scotsman. But you must leave. The pucelle lodged in town last night, but she will be riding out this morning to hear Mass before we advance to Melun.'

'And I must be out of the way before the saintly Maid arrives? Oh, you obviously value me highly!'

'Do you expect to be valued at all?' he asked, genuinely amazed.

She flounced out angrily without replying, and sulked on the edge of the clearing.

Two of the other girls tumbled out of a nearby tent and ran across to her.

Bertha knew the one with red hair was a Parisian who had turned harlot after her sweetheart was killed.

'When other girls are bereaved,' Aimee had giggled, 'They go into convents. I have chosen a different profession and follow it with equal dedication.'

The other girl was dark-skinned and silent, for she spoke only the dialect of her tribe. She had identified herself as Alianor and Bertha guessed she had broken some tribal law and been cast out by her people.

'Did your man tell you that we must leave before the pucelle comes?' Aimee asked, indignantly.

'He hid me away as if I were a bad smell,' Bertha muttered. 'I'm not used to such treatment, I can tell you! Does he imagine I'll put up with it!'

'If the pucelle finds you, there'll be trouble,' Aimee warned.

'A fig for the pucelle! Who is she to stop us from giving comfort to poor suffering soldiers who may be killed in a day or two? If the men go to Melun, we go also.'

'How?'

'We'll hide at the back of the supply wagon. Nobody will see us among the grain. After the battle, we join the winning side, and no girl dressed up as a man is going to stop me!'

Bertha spoke with more courage than she felt. Camp-followers did not ride into battle, but hid in the woods and fields around until it was safe to go down. But supply wagons were often attacked or set on fire. Bertha tossed her head.

'If you're afraid, stay behind,' she said, 'but I, for one, intend to prove that the holy Maid isn't the only woman who can ride into battle!'

She regretted her words later when she lay in the wagon, wedged between two bales of straw and listened to the sounds of fighting all around. During a lull, she ventured to pull back the canvas sides of the vehicle and peeped out. The field was a confusion of men and horses, some of them lying dead or groaning, others grouped about the leaders of the various divisions.

'What's happening? Can't we jump out and get to safety among the trees?'

'We can't! They've drawn up the wagons too far in the open.'

'I've had every tooth in my head shaken out of its socket,' Aimee complained. 'I don't know why I agreed to come. Why couldn't we have stayed at Lagny and waited for them to return?'

'When you've been at this as long as I have, you'll learn there's good pickings to be had on a battlefield,' Bertha answered, and dived back into the security of the hay as the dull roar of the cannon began again.

The shouting and shooting went on for an eternity, and there was a roar of flame and smoke as the wagon in front of them caught fire. Aimee was moaning softly, and swearing to renounce all men if the Blessed Virgin would only condescend to spare her. The gypsy girl sat quietly, with her hands in her lap, and an avid look on her face. From time to time, Bertha risked a quick glance outside, but the smoke from the burning wagon made her eyes sting, and the cacophony of sounds hurt her ears.

The silence descended gradually, so that they became aware of it by degrees.

Bertha pushed aside the canvas, and looked out at the littered ground, where green grass had been ploughed up by hoofs. Some soldiers were putting out various small fires by emptying the contents of leather buckets over them. Two horses with their undersides shot away were moaning as they waited for the slaughterer's knife.

'Who won?' Aimee was hissing.

'The pucelle's men,' Bertha said, as she let herself down to the ground, stepped cautiously over a man with half his head blown off, and watched the fleur-du-lys being run up over the drawbridge.

Aimee was standing beside her, with fingers to her nose. 'Faugh! What an awful stench! I wish blood didn't smell quite so much like blood!' she said, fastidiously.

Alianor grinned and stuck out her foot so that Aimee, tripping, sprawled in the mud. She came up, swearing, with all pretence of gentility gone, and the two of them were soon rolling on the ground.

Bertha walked away from them, ignoring the brown-clad foot soldiers who were, she knew, paid after the battle. She paused briefly by a young captain who lay on his side, looking peacefully asleep, with an arrow in his chest. There was a handsome brooch pinned to his sleeve, and she fastened it carefully to her bodice, then moved on slowly. The next body yielded several pieces of silver, and the next a prettily embroidered sash.

Out of the corner of her eye, she saw that her two companions had ceased quarrelling and were talking to a couple of the fire-fighters who had put down their buckets and were laughing heartily.

Three more soldiers came through the open gates of the town, and Bertha, recognizing her companion of the previous night, ran towards him.

'Bertha! What the devil are you doing here?'

'I've been here all the time,' she said, pertly. 'You didn't think I'd run away so tamely, did you?'

'What has he got that we haven't got?' one of the other men demanded.

'Well, now,' Bertha drawled, 'I don't know you well enough yet to say if you've got it or not!'

'Then we'll remedy that!' The archer pulled Bertha towards him and kissed her.

'Kissing makes me thirsty,' she complained.

'The taverns will quench that. Come on!'

He had his arm around her waist and was pulling her towards the open gates. Half a dozen dispirited goddams were being led out under guard. Behind them, a couple of city whores were swaggering, with captured helmets on their heads and bodices unlaced. Alianor and Aimee were coming across the slope with their escorts. They had filled the leather buckets with ale and were drinking as they walked, with a good deal of spilling, splashing and laughter.

'We won! We bloody well won!' One of the men whooped with delight, tried to execute a cartwheel and sat down abruptly pulling Aimee across him.

Bertha pressed close against the soldier's chest, felt rather than saw the alien presence. The armoured figure who stood looking at them said nothing, but her gaze seemed to have frozen the men into immobility, like figures on a frieze.

Aimee's giggles trailed away, and Alianor made the sign against the evil eye.

'God have mercy on us!' whispered one of the men, 'but 'tis the Pucelle herself!'

Bertha raised her head and stared at the Maid. The pucelle had taken off her helmet, but her sword was still in her hand, and beads of perspiration were rolling down her face.

'Is this how you give thanks to God for our victory to-day?' Joan asked.

'We were only having a bit of fun,' one of the men said.

'I like not your idea of *fun*!' Joan said, contemptuously.

'I wasn't doing any harm,' Aimee wailed, but Joan turned on her immediately.

'Women of your kind do harm wherever they go! You are like carrion crows, feeding on the bodies of the dead. You are like magpies, stealing the gold that belongs to others. Men who fight in a just cause must go into battle with their hearts high and uplifted, but you drag men down, making animals of them. You sell your bodies and bring shame to honest women and disease to honest men. I will have no harlots in my armies nor in my towns!'

Alianor had slunk away and Aimee was sobbing wildly. The soldiers were looking at the floor as if they wished it would swallow them up, and the city whores were open-mouthed with terrified astonishment.

Bertha tossed back her mane of hair and spoke defiantly.

'Carrion crows and magpies, are we? And what are you, I'd like to know! At least *we* give pleasure to the men before *you* send them out to die. And as for bringing shame upon honest women, I've yet to hear of an honest woman who dressed up in men's garments and rode about like a boy. It's my belief that you're not a real girl at all, but an odd creature of no sex such as are shown at freak shows!'

Joan's face was so white that the sprinkling of freckles across her nose stood out sharply.

'I order you to leave this place,' she said, thickly. 'In the name of Our Lord, I order you to go!'

'A fig for your Lord!' Bertha shouted. 'No strumpet in chain mail tells me what to do! Are the rest of you witless that you say nothing? Are you all fools to take the orders of a thing in whose mouth the name of God is foul?'

She might have said more, but there was no time. Joan had lunged forward, beating the woman about the head and shoulders with the flat of her sword. The others had fallen back with exclamations of horror, and Bertha was vainly trying to shield herself with her hands and arms.

There was a sharp crack as the sword broke in two pieces, and a louder crack as a streak of lightning ran up the sky and drops of rain began to fall.

Joan had stooped to pick up the two lengths of shining metal. Bertha took one look at the Maid's set face, then picked up her skirts and ran, tripping over discarded weapons as she went. Behind her, the other women rushed, too, with squeals of hysteria.

Joan took no further notice of any of them. She was walking away, striding with bent head beneath the walls of the town. The soldiers turned towards the gates, muttering uneasily among themselves.

Joan moved quickly but the rain was falling steadily by the time she gained the hill overlooking Melun, and from the east came ever-increasing growls of thunder, while the sky was the colour of lead.

From the hill she could look down over the city walls, and beyond to the trampled meadow where men and horses, wagons and weapons were diminished by distance to the size of dolls.

Joan knelt down, fitting together her broken sword, running her fingers across the jagged scar that now rendered it useless.

'You broke your vow, Pucelle,' the voice said gravely.

'I know it.'

The Maid looked up at the figure of her saint and spoke humbly, but St Catherine's stern expression did not relax.

'You vowed never to strike a blow with the sword.'

'I lost my temper,' Joan said humbly.

'The sword will not be mended,' went on the inexorable voice, 'for its power has fled. You must, in future, use another weapon.'

'How can I fight on?'

'Because it is the Lord's will that you complete your mission.'

'To unite all France?'

'Who are you to say when your mission will be ended?' came the voice again. 'You are here to obey. But one thing I am permitted to tell you. Before St John's Day you will be taken by the enemy.'

'A prisoner? In the hands of the goddams? Dear God, but they will burn me as a witch. Let me be killed in battle instead. I could not endure captivity. I have lived as a soldier has lived. Grant me the right to die as a soldier dies.'

Joan stretched out her hands pleadingly, but the beautiful face was cold.

'Who are you to choose the manner of your death?' asked the icy voice.

'Then tell me at what hour I shall be taken.'

'So that you can thwart the Will of God by remaining at home on that day? Do you think we cannot read the drift of your thoughts? We know every shade of your mind. And you will not escape the destiny intended for you, unless you disobey God and lose your soul.'

'But am I to die at the hands of my enemies?'

'It is not for you to ask questions, Pucelle, but to accept bravely what is sent.'

The voice was fading and the figure was receding and she was alone again on the bare hillside.

She got to her feet tiredly and started down the steep hill towards the city. A little group of soldiers ran to meet her as she neared the gates.

'Pucelle, another miracle has been wrought in your name!' one of them babbled, excitedly.

'What miracle? What nonsense are you babbling about?'

'Pucelle, is it not true that word was brought to you at Lagny of a child that had died before it could be baptized?'

'Aye, it was so. The little babe never cried but died unchristened.'

'And did you not pray for the baby?'

'I knelt down and prayed when I heard of the matter. So did other young girls of the town. What of it?'

'A runner is here from Lagny. He brings news that the baby lived again. The child was black in the face and laid in its coffin ready to be placed in the ground, and it drew breath and wailed faint as a kitten's mew. The priest baptized the child at once, and when an hour had passed, it died again.'

'Your prayers have brought eternal heaven to a human soul,' cried one of the men. 'It must be wonderful to be such a powerful friend of the Lord!'

'Do you think so?' She looked at the soldier in amazement.

'You are the Pucelle. If it was your wish, God would strike the goddams dead with one bolt of lightning!'

'It is I who must obey,' she said, sombrely. 'God gives the victories, but we must fight the battles!'

'Not with that sword!'

The soldier drew the broken pieces from her grasp.

'It is the Pucelle's magic sword,' whispered another. 'It is the sword of Saint Michael!'

They stared at her, troubled and dismayed.

'I broke my promise,' she said, 'and the sword is now useless.'

'Then we must mend it. We must change the omens.'

'No armourer can rivet that together,' Joan declared. 'But

it doesn't matter. I can give as good buffets with another weapon.'

'But if its power is gone?'

They crowded about her, looking tense and afraid.

'Do you think all of God's power is contained in one sword?' Joan enquired. 'We will have good victories yet, and I will lead you into battle again. Now we will go into the church and give thanks for today's success.'

Minguet came forward with her horse and handed her banner up to her. Lightning flashed over the turrets of the gate, and many of the citizens had hurried for shelter. D'Aulun had fallen in behind her, and the ever faithful Minguet was beaming brightly.

For a brief instant, desolation closed down around her again. She looked forlornly at the people rushing forward to cheer. If only d'Alençon or Dunois were there, but they were in Normandy and there were few of her old friends left.

Then a man pushed his way to the front and shouted, 'God bless you, Pucelle! I was at Orleans and Jargeau with you, and will follow wherever you lead.'

Her spirit lifted. The King might sulk at Gien and listen as de Chartres and La Tremouille dripped their poison into his ears. Her captains might be scattered by the fortunes of war. But the soldiers whom she bullied and scolded still loved her, and she had captured another town for Charles.

She raised her head proudly as they rode beneath the arches. But above the cheering, the voices sounded.

'Before St John's Day comes, you will be taken by the enemy.'

Overhead the thunder rolled.

CHAPTER NINE

COMPIEGNE, MAY, 1430

IT had been, thought Simon, a hell of a winter. To begin with, he had been trapped into wedlock by a girl with blue eyes and a mouth made for kissing. It had never occurred to him that he might be married one day.

More than a year had passed since he had caught sight of Jacques Alain at Nancy, and that glimpse had been enough to send him scurrying deeper into Burgundy, fearing, as he went, that his benefactor's hearty kindness would reach out and seize him. He had been near starving when he met Rosine and she had given him some bread and some figs from her basket, and helped him to limp to the wooden shack where she lived.

He had slept heavily that night and in the morning Rosine had given him eggs and cheese, and taken him to the garrison where he had enlisted as an archer in the service of the bastard of Wendomme. It was a small garrison where they needed recruits and didn't ask too many questions about a man's past. Wendomme himself was in the service of Jean de Luxemburg, and took a pride in training the men under his command to shoot straight and bear hardship without grumbling.

Nobody, Simon learned, contradicted Wendomme if he wished to keep a whole skin. Under the Burgundians' rough and ready treatment, he shed years of undisciplined wandering and learned to take orders without question. There were times when he considered running away again, but then Wendomme would clap him on the back, declaring,

'We'll make a soldier of you yet, my lad!'

And there was Rosine, with her tear-drenched eyes and slender hands and pretty smile. Rosine was, like himself, an orphan and earned her living by sewing and cooking for the officers' wives who were too grand to soil their own hands.

She was a familiar figure around the garrison and the soldiers respected her, recognizing in her an innocence that hardship couldn't corrupt. She was not yet sixteen, yet she had kept herself in respectable independence for nearly four years, since her father had died.

If Simon left, what would happen to Rosine? His common sense told him that she would continue to live as she had lived before he came, but he remained in Wendomme's service; and when the long hours of drilling and discipline were over, he would hurry along the forest road to meet her.

'Girls like Rosine are the kind you marry,' Wendomme said bluntly, one day. 'You had better wed the girl. Don't gape at me, man. It's time you took a wife.'

'She may not have me,' Simon said, hopefully.

'I've spoken to her and she's willing, so we'll call the priest and have the knot legally tied.'

Wendomme stomped out of the guardroom, and Gaston burst out laughing.

'The bastard values you and knows you're less likely to stray if you have a wife!'

'I would have liked to choose my own woman,' Simon muttered.

'You'll do well if you bear one thing in mind,' Gaston chuckled. 'When Wendomme tells you to attack, you attack; when he tells you it's time to get wedded, you get wedded; and when he tells you it's time to die, you say your prayers and fall on your sword.'

Simon had not meant to marry, but he had been married. He had meant to leave Rosine behind when they marched over the border into France. But Wendomme allowed his men to take their wives on campaign, and Rosine had stuffed her belongings into a large canvas bag and ridden behind him without complaint over the rough ground.

Simon admired her spirit and welcomed her soft arms

when they lay together at night, but her love was a bond-
age more difficult to bear than the reiterated commands of
Wendomme.

She asked him if he had ever loved another woman and
he was able to answer truthfully that he had not, and was
glad she took for granted the fact that he loved her, for he
would have been hard-pressed to put into words the feelings of irritation and affection that filled him when he saw
her standing by the horse with the ridiculous canvas bag
in her arms and her wedding ring glinting on her finger.

But they had travelled slowly, bogged down in the mud
of the February thaw, lashed by rain, preyed upon by the
robber bands that infested the highways.

Now they were camped at Margny on the rising ground
across the river from Compiegne. The whole area was
dotted with English and Burgundian divisions, in preparation for the big offensive against Compiegne.

'The position is clear,' said Wendomme briskly, as his
men squatted around him.

He took a stick and engraved as he talked, cutting a
rough map in the black earth of the river-bank.

'This river is called the Oise, and this bridge leads to
Compiegne. The main force is with the Duke of Burgundy
at Caudun, waiting to cross the Aronde. Five miles down
river at Vedette, our gallant allies,' he paused to spit, 'the
English, are encamped. There are not many of them, as
most have been held back at Calais to escort the little King
Henry to Paris. Now, five miles up river at Claroix is my
overlord, and yours, Jean de Luxemburg. He will be riding
over later to give me his personal instructions. Meanwhile,
we hold back and wait. We will occupy the time by erect-
ing a stockade, and by making sure that none of the
pucelle's men get across the bridge.'

'Is the pucelle at Compiegne?'

There was a startled murmur, and Wendomme grinned.

'You've heard the rumours about the invincible d'Arc,
I see. Well, she's not so unbeatable now. She couldn't take

Paris and she couldn't take La Charite, and she'll not hold Compiegne for very long. Her forces are loyal, I'm told, but she's waiting for reinforcements, and she can't rely too heavily on the goodwill of Compiegne. So we needn't worry about the pucelle, although I'm told there's a reward of three thousand livres for the man who captures her—alive.'

'Three thousand livres! Oh, Simon, think what we could do with all that money!'

Rosine had crept up to the circle and rested her head against his shoulder.

'What would *you* do with it?' he asked her, moving towards the fire where their bedrolls were spread.

'I'd buy your discharge from the service of Wendomme so that you could be your own man, and I'd build a house with stone walls, and a garden at the side where I could grow herbs. And I would buy a pink dress, and a fine white shawl for the baby.'

'What baby?'

'Oh, Simon, I had not meant to tell you so soon, but I am with child.'

'God Almighty, no! Rosine, you can't have a baby when we're on campaign!'

'The baby will not be born for many months,' she said, and hugged him tightly. 'Wendomme is a good man, but he would not have let me travel with the army if he had known about the child. Don't be cross, Simon! I wanted you to be happy about the baby. Aren't you happy to have a family of your own?'

'Very happy,' Simon said gloomily, and added another burden to the ones he already reluctantly carried.

In the morning he had scant attention to pay to his wife, for he was kicked awake by a burly sergeant who ordered him to get on his damned feet, and look lively, because the pucelle was riding across the bridge and the men who were supposed to guard the bridge had flung away their weapons and scattered.

'Oh, darling, do be careful,' Rosine was begging. 'And

don't try to capture the pucelle by yourself. We really don't need the money.'

She would have kissed him and clung to him, but he pushed her aside and charged out with the rest, fitting an arrow to his bow as he ran.

There were, he calculated, no more than two or three hundred of the enemy, but they had gained the bridge and were fighting their way, foot by foot, up the slopes.

Simon dodged behind a bush and dropped to one knee, measuring the distance between him and the cavalry bunched at the bridge. There was an odd, uneasy silence, broken by harsh breathing and the neigh of a horse.

Then a woman's voice called out, 'Forward! France for God and King Charles!'

The horses thundered up the banks and the arrows rained down from above. The enemy ranks splintered in confusion. Men were fleeing back across the bridge, slipping and sliding on the wet planks, flailing their arms wildly in the river.

The woman's voice rose again, 'Turn back and fight! Fifty thousand angels will guard you!'

But the retreat continued, while the Burgundian archers raised themselves from their knees and advanced slowly and relentlessly towards the bridge.

The French were aiming fire-faggots, pausing briefly as they fled to open the gates of Compiegne. Most of the flaming torches fell short of their intended targets, or spluttered out harmlessly in the deep puddles; but two or three found their mark and a thin line of flame ran along the edges of the wooden stockade. There was the cracking of wood, and the squealing of women as they tried to beat down the flames with their shawls.

Simon dropped to the ground, feigning death as a French captain galloped past, slashing with his broad sword at anything that moved.

Somebody was calling his name, screaming it above all the din. Rosine was running down towards him from the blazing stockade, crying out his name over and over again, running towards him with her arms outstretched, running and falling amid the trampling hoofs, and rising and falling again.

She looked very small and curiously boneless, with her bare feet sticking up out of the mud and one arm torn from its socket. He knelt down by her and her blue eyes looked up at him out of her shattered face. Then she smiled at him with terrible, tugging love, and died without saying anything. A few yards away, trodden into the soil, lay her silly canvas bag.

'The enemy are in full retreat. The pucelle cannot hold them!'

The words gave him a furious joy. He had risen and was running again, heedless of fireballs and culverins, flinging away his bow and stabbing fiercely with his sharp-honed knife.

The pucelle had reached the meadows and was fighting to defend her rear troops. There were two or three men still with her, but gradually she was being borne away by the crowds of Burgundians. Voices on all sides were crying out, 'Yield to me! Yield to me!'

Simon had reached her side and could feel his heart hammering over the searing pain in his ribs. He reached up and pulled her down, holding her tightly while he forced his exhausted lungs to breathe deeply, giving him the strength to cry, 'The pucelle is mine! I claim the pucelle!'

They were pulling her between them as if she were the most valuable prize in the world, but Wendomme was slashing his way towards them and others of his troop were holding back the circle of would-be captors.

'Burgundians! I'll have your heads!'

Joan was screaming at them, with her arms pinioned and a ferocious scowl on her face. Nearby a French captain was calling, 'Have courage! Have courage!'

'Have courage yourself, d'Aulun, for you need it more than I do!' Joan retorted.

'She fights like a wildcat!' exclaimed Wendomme admiringly. 'Put her back on her horse, lad, and we'll hand her over to the Duke.'

'But the reward? The three thousand livres?'

'Rumour, boy. Mere rumour!' Wendomme grinned, seizing Joan by her wrists and pushing her ahead of him.

'But you said there was a reward!'

'I tell an awful lot of lies,' Wendomme chuckled. 'There may be a bag of silver for you in it, but I'll make no promises. Now get back to your post. There's work to be done.'

'But the money? What of the money?'

It was useless. Wendomme had moved away, and Simon was being squeezed to the fringe of the group.

A young boy, with tears running down his face, was riding towards the town. Simon pulled out his knife again, but killing the youngster required too much energy, and he was drained of all passion.

He put his knife back in his sheath, and walked towards the stockade.

BEAUREVOIR, AUGUST, 1430

'But how could you be so foolish as to think you could escape in such a fashion?' d'Aulun scolded.

'It's a prisoner's duty to try to escape,' Joan argued.

'But not by jumping from the top of a high tower! You might have broken your neck.'

'Well, it was better than sitting still, doing nothing,' Joan retorted.

The long idle summer in the kindly captivity of the Burgundians had not, d'Aulun noticed, abated her fighting spirit.

After they had been taken, d'Aulun had suffered agonies of anxiety concerning the welfare of the pucelle. He had been receiving treatment for a wounded foot and had imagined Joan being subjected to every sort of indignity; but when he was permitted to rejoin her, he found her settled in a comfortable room with three young women to wait upon her. The women were so charmed by the important prisoner that, when the Duke of Burgundy arrived, to collect Joan and hand over the sum of six thousand francs to Jean de Luxemburg, they burst into lamentations, begging their master not to dishonour himself.

She had been taken up river to the castle of Beaurevoir, near Saint Quentin, and the short journey had become quite a triumphal procession, with the ladies of Luxemburg's household piling their captive with gifts of fruit and flowers.

At Beaurevoir, they might, d'Aulun considered, have been very content. The Duke of Burgundy proved to be, not an ogre, but a handsome old man who addressed Joan as princess and paid her compliments on her fighting skill.

Food and wine were plentiful, a musician was brought to entertain her, and she was allowed to walk about on the flat roof of the tower whenever she pleased.

D'Aulun would not readily forget the spasm of horror that had gripped him when he had looked over the parapet and seen her lying motionless on the cobbles below. It was a wonder she had not been killed. As it was, she had a lump on the back of her head like a pigeon's egg, and a headache to match to judge from her groans when she recovered consciousness.

'They will accuse you of trying to commit suicide,' he said, now.

'To commit——d'Aulun, I would never do such a thing!'

'*I* know that, and *you* know that, but do the Burgundians! They will think of it as another proof of your wickedness.'

'I'm not interested in what the Burgundians think!' she said sulkily.

'Did your saints tell you to jump?'

She shook her head. 'My saints were angry when I tried

166

to escape. They told me that I must be patient.'

'Then they obviously know you are to be ransomed by the King!' D'Aulun exclaimed. 'There is hope yet, Pucelle, for the Duke would have handed you over to the English by now, if he meant you harm.'

'He's waiting to find out who is offering the biggest ransom for me,' she replied. 'And my King has very little money.'

'Then he'll have to pawn the crown jewels again,' d'Aulun said heartlessly. 'He's done it before, for lesser causes. Even if he does not, the citizens of Orleans will raise money for their Maid.'

'They think well of me there, don't they?' She cheered up immediately and began talking with animation. 'And I love Orleans, for there I had my first victory. I want to settle there eventually, when the troubles are over. I told you that I had bought a little house for my mother. Now that my brother, Jacquemin, is dead, Domremy holds sadness for her. She and my father deserve some leisure after a lifetime of hard work. Did you know I had received word from my brothers? The Duke of Burgundy was good enough to enquire for news of them. Pierre has gone home, to help on the farm. And Jean has gone to Vaucouleurs and entered the service of Sir Robert de Baudicourt. I wish I could see Sir Robert again. I would tease him by reminding him of the time he called me a great pest!'

'We will visit him together when our ransoms have arrived,' d'Aulun said.

'Do you truly believe the King will send sufficient money for me?'

'If he does not,' the captain retorted, 'then the centuries will cry aloud his treachery. Until you came, he had no throne and his Kingdom was shrunken and in jeopardy. Oh, he may not listen to you as attentively as he used to do, but when you are in real danger, he must exert himself on your behalf, if only to save his own honour!'

He broke off as a polite knock sounded on the door. A

moment later, Philip of Burgundy entered the sunlit apartment, bowing low with his usual courtesy.

'I hope I find you quite recovered from your fall, Pucelle,' he began.

'Perfectly recovered, and longing for some exercise, my lord.'

'Ah, you would like a swift horse, I daresay, to carry you eastward to your own village, or south to Orleans! You must think me very foolish! Are you also well again, d'Aulun? I was told your foot was troubling you.'

'It aches in wet weather, my lord Duke.'

'I've brought some apples for you, Joan. A basket of them waits for you outside the door. I was told you were fond of the fruit.'

'But you didn't come merely to deliver apples and enquire about my health!' Joan said, sharply.

'I came to tell you that d'Aulun's ransom has arrived. You will be granted a safe conduct into your own territory.'

'And?'

Joan had sat bolt upright on the window-seat.

'I wish the tidings I bring were more hopeful, Pucelle. Believe me, but there is no personal malice in this.'

'I know you have treated me with a chivalry I did not expect from a Burgundian,' she repeated. 'But I also know that to you I am not a human being, but a piece of merchandise to be handed to the highest bidder. So come to the point, my lord, and tell me who offers the most money for Joan the Maid.'

'The English have offered ten thousand livres for you, Joan.'

'I did not think there was so much money even in England,' d'Aulun exclaimed.

'There is not,' Philip answered, wryly. 'They have raised the sum by imposing a tax on Normandy. Apparently a friend of yours, d'Alençon has been trying to raise money himself in that quarter, but the Duchy is mainly English in sympathy.'

'What would the English do with Joan?' d'Aulun asked.

'That is not my concern,' Philip answered, stiffly, 'but I am assured she would receive a fair trial.'

'Trial for what? She has broken no English laws!'

'She might be tried for heresy, captain.'

'Joan a heretic? I never heard such a preposterous——'

'Be quiet, d'Aulun!' Joan said, sharply. She looked up at the Duke and asked, 'You say the goddams offered you ten thousand livres for me? What of my own King? How much has he offered?'

'Charles has offered nothing, Joan. He merely sent his regrets that you had been taken.'

D'Aulun, forgetting his aching foot, had sprung up, indignant and incredulous. The Duke of Burgundy watched his prisoner curiously, wondering how she would react to this betrayal which had shocked even his mercenary soul.

She sat for a moment, looking at her clasped hands.

'It was a very little Kingdom when I first began,' she said slowly, and began to weep as if she would never stop.

ROUEN, FEBRUARY, 1431

'But if you do not learn to draw your bow straight, my liege, how can you expect to rule your domains?'

'I would rule with love, uncle, not by the power of the sword.'

John, Duke of Bedford, bit his lip and frowned down at the velvet-clad figure standing before him. Nine-year-old Henry, King of England and of France, was the gentlest and most sweet-tempered of nephews, but monarchs needed strength of character and mental vigour. Henry's occasional outbursts of obstinate rage were unfortunately more reminiscent of his maternal grandfather, the lunatic Charles VI, than of his father, the warlike Henry V.

'When you have conquered, my liege,' Bedford said, coaxingly, 'you can afford to rule with love. But you will, one day lead armies into battle, and so you must not neglect your Knightly exercises now.'

'Yes, uncle!'

Henry sighed, wondering if he dare terminate the interview. Theoretically he could tell the Duke of Bedford to leave the room, but he was not at all sure that he would be obeyed, and it was best not to risk a slight to his dignity.

Sometimes, he longed to run about freely like his half-brothers, Edmund and Jasper, and little Owen. The three little boys ran races up and down the corridors of White-hall, and sprawled about on the grass, dirtying their clothes. But it was explained to him that, while it was all very well for the Tudor boys to roll around like puppies, he was the King and must never appear at a disadvantage.

More than anything in the world, Henry looked forward to his brief, annual visits to Ludlow Castle where his mother lived with her second husband, Owen Tudor.

There had been, Henry knew, a great deal of trouble over that second marriage. Nobody had known anything about it until an official of the Privy Council, paying a courtesy visit to the queen-dowager in her retirement, had found Queen Katharine in her solar with her red-headed attendant lying across her lap, and three red-headed babies in the nursery.

Of course, Henry reflected, it had been very shocking of Maman to wed without the consent of the Council, but he could not help liking his stepfather, even if the Tudors were Welsh upstarts who had sold cattle along the borders of Pembroke. Owen Tudor paid his small stepson all the homage insisted upon by the Dukes, but when they were on holiday at Ludlow, formalities were relaxed, and Henry didn't think it beneath his dignity to climb up on Owen's knee and listen to thrilling legends about the land of Wales while Queen Katharine sat near, smiling and talking in her husky little voice.

'You are dreaming again, my liege,' Bedford said severely.

'I was thinking about my Coronation,' Henry said, quickly. 'I cannot remember when I was crowned as King of England.'

'Indeed, no, for you were only a babe of nine months and had to be held on your mother's knee,' Bedford agreed. 'But when you are crowned and anointed at Paris, you will be fully aware of the deep significance of the ceremony.'

Henry sighed again, wondering if any of them guessed how irritable and bored he became when he had to sit still for long periods. To bury one's nose in a book or hunch over an interesting game of chess was one thing, but to sit on a hard throne with heavy vestments dragging him down—the mere thought of it made him feel sick.

'I don't like France,' he complained, petulantly. 'I wish we could get the Coronation over, and go home again.'

'Not like France? Oh, my liege, how can you say that when so many men have laid down their lives to secure this territory for you?' Bedford reproached.

Henry wriggled uncomfortably, conscious that he had said the wrong thing again. But he had been wretchedly sick during the rough Channel crossing, and at Calais it had rained and his favourite dog had caught cold and died.

He liked Rouen even less, for it was full of common, rough-looking peasants who swarmed through the narrow streets, crowding about him when he rode out on his pony and having to be beaten back by his guards.

Rouen was full of guards. Armoured figures kept watch on every gate, spilled out of every doorway, lined the walls of the town and the battlements of the castles.

They were here, not only to guard the King, but to ensure that the witch girl would not be rescued. When Henry thought of the pucelle, he felt very cross indeed. If it had not been for her, the troubles would not have broken out again and he would have gone straight to Paris to be crowned, and had been back in England again by now.

But, even after her capture, there had been endless

delays. The Duke of Burgundy wouldn't hand her over until he'd received his money, and when she was finally in English hands, they had had to spend more money on bribes to the churchmen who would try her as a heretic.

'If the woman from Lorraine is really a devil-woman,' Henry asked, 'why do we have to pay the judges money to find her guilty?'

'My liege, the woman will receive a fair trial, and be found guilty at the end of it!'

'That doesn't sound very logical,' Henry said, doubtfully.

'It's a matter of politics,' his uncle said, firmly. 'Be assured, Majesty, that the girl condemns herself as a heretic every time she speaks. There have been ten sittings of the tribunal already, and she has said enough to be found guilty a dozen times over. And this chatter has not caused me to forget that you still have your archery practice to fulfil.'

'I'm coming, uncle.'

Henry picked up his bow wearily and followed his formidable relative down to the butts.

It was chilly in the open air, and he sneezed miserably eyeing the target with watering eyes.

'Your father and I used to have fine contests when we were lads,' Bedford was saying heartily. 'He was the finest sportsman of his time.'

And the finest dancer, and the finest musician, and the finest King, Henry thought gloomily. All the actions of his short life had been measured against the exploits of his father, and he didn't believe he would ever achieve half of what was expected of him.

His arrow fell short of the target.

'Well done, my liege,' the Duke cried encouragingly. 'The strings of the bow are not yet supple enough, I fear. Fit another arrow and stand closer.'

The second arrow just found its mark, and Bedford clapped loudly, calling to the Earl of Warwick who had strolled up.

'An excellent shot! Don't you think so, my lord? If the wind had not caused the arrow to swerve, we might have hit the centre!'

'His Majesty's marksmanship has greatly improved,' Warwick remarked, cordially.

Henry wished they would say what they were really thinking, instead of forever flattering and encouraging. But in Court circles nobody ever spoke the truth.

Then he remembered having seen a copy of a letter dictated by the witch girl, Joan, to his uncle. Some of the phrases had stuck in his mind.

'You so-called Regent of France. Go away for God's sake back to your own country, else the Maid will visit you to your great detriment.'

The notion of calling his uncle to account in such a fashion tickled his fancy so much that he laughed aloud. The Earl of Warwick looked at him gravely.

'Torture is not a matter for mirth, my liege,' he said, severely.

'We were discussing this question of having the pucelle tortured,' Bedford said.

'I wasn't listening, uncle.'

'My dear nephew, I have told you before that it is necessary to pay close attention to everything that is said in your presence. We were talking of the judges' decision not to use torture against the witch. The Earl agrees with me that she does not deserve such mercy. A taste of the rack might make her more amenable to reason.'

Henry's delicate skin had paled. He hated the idea of pain for himself and for others, and there was something dreadful in the thought of putting a girl on the rack, even if she had sold her soul to the devil.

'I think we ought to go in and pray for her soul,' he shivered.

'Your Majesty has a gentle heart,' Warwick said, casting an exasperated glance at Bedford.

As they crossed the outer fosse on their way back to the

royal apartments, Henry paused briefly to watch a small group of soldiers marching in ragged formation along the lower path. There was a brown-clad figure in their midst and the soldiers were talking loudly and gesturing. Then the figure whipped round and caught one of the men a sharp blow across the mouth with her chained wrist.

So that was the notorious pucelle! The King leaned over the parapet and stared at the girl, wishing she would look up so that he could see her face clearly. But his companions had stopped also.

'Sire, it is not fitting that an anointed monarch should look upon a creature of hell!' Bedford exclaimed.

Henry allowed himself to be escorted to his apartments, and went at once to the private chapel leading from his bedroom, where he sank to his knees and applied himself to his devotions with a concentration he never showed at archery practice.

'He is truly pious,' Bedford whispered.

'A sensitive child,' Warwick agreed.

The two men watched the little King sombrely, fearing the future.

'When the pucelle is burned, we will be able to dictate what terms we choose to the de Valois,' Bedford murmured.

'Then we must arrange the Coronation ceremonies,' Warwick said.

Before the altar, the voice of Henry VI rose in prayer.

'Protect all men from the lures of Satan, and grant eternal rest to the souls of the faithful. Amen.'

CHINON, MAY, 1431

The orchards and fields of Touraine were green and white tapestries laid over the earth. At his favourite palace, Charles de Valois walked in the gardens with his mistress, and wished they might remain there for ever.

'Then I would grow fat as your mother did, and you would not love me,' Agnes protested.

'Don't speak of my mother,' Charles said, nervously, hating to be reminded of the beautiful Queen Isabel, made gross and twisted by disease. –

'Then what shall we discuss? Shall we talk about current events? Do you want to read again the despatches from Rouen? The Pucelle has refused to submit to the Church Militant, but appeals still to the Church Triumphant in Heaven.'

'I don't want to hear about Joan.'

'Why not? Does it hurt your feelings to be reminded about her? It is almost a year since she was taken, and it is said she has been ill-treated in prison, since the goddams bought her.'

'I said I didn't want to talk about it.'

Charles shook away her detaining hand from his arm and walked away, but Agnes followed him, lifting her heavy scarlet robes and treading daintily on her golden slippers.

'They have threatened her with rape and torture,' Agnes persisted, 'and loaded her with chains and refused to allow her to hear Mass. And she has refused to say one word against you. I would call that loyalty, wouldn't you?'

'Call it what you choose, but don't badger me,' he cried. 'On all sides, I am blamed because I didn't leap on a white charger and gallop to the Maid's rescue. Well, I cut a sorry figure on a horse! And if I had offered money for her return, the English would have offered more! I told Jean de Metz and d'Alençon the same thing. Dunois too! Yet still they hammer at me, day after day. Why can't they all leave me alone? Why must they go on, and on, and on? Don't they realize that there was nothing I could do?'

'You could have made a small gesture,' Agnes said, sadly. 'It would have cost you nothing.'

'They will give her a merciful sentence. Her judges are churchmen, not monsters,' he argued. 'Massieu, and Ladvenu, and de la Fontaine, and Houppeville are most favourably inclined towards her.'

'And de la Fontaine has been dismissed for venturing to give Joan advice, and Houppeville is in prison for criticizing Bishop Cauchon. And Bishop Cauchon will never forgive the Maid for driving him from his see at Beauvais. You cannot expect justice from such a man. And the rest of them have either been bribed by the goddams, or are too cowed to speak.'

'You should have gone to Rouen yourself,' Charles snapped. 'You would have been a most powerful advocate, for a woman who would not even be presented to you when she came to court!'

'You're angry with me because I show you the truth,' Agnes said.

'Who knows *what* the truth is?' Charles asked wearily. 'Do you? I don't! Did Joan carry truth in her? Was she really obeying the commands of God when she came to Chinon? Or do her voices come from some dark region? And if her voices did come from Heaven, why did she sometimes disobey them? She has said that she disobeyed them, you know!'

Agnes watched him as he paced along the narrow path, between the trim hedges, where fruit blossom lay thickly sprinkled. As he talked, he took on an air of spurious authority. Soon, thought Agnes, he will convince himself that it is not he who betrayed Joan, but Joan who betrayed him.

There should have been another King upon the throne, her thoughts ran on. A stronger, wiser man would have been more worthy, but then I might not have loved him and he certainly wouldn't have loved me.

'Shall we go in?' she asked, aloud. 'I would like to send for the musicians and have them play something bright and gay.'

'So that we may cast off our dismal mood!' he cried, eagerly. 'Oh, there will be good times yet, my darling, and you will have those emeralds that I promised you. And we won't quarrel again. It is senseless to quarrel when we love each other so much!'

Smiling, she agreed and they moved in outward harmony to the door of his private apartments.

CHAPTER TEN

ROUEN, MAY, 1431

'A N D what business might you have in Rouen, my pretty?'

The woman at the gate pushed back her heavy yellow hair and smiled up at the guard.

'I came to visit my aged father,' she said, coyly.

'The only father you ever had, had a serpent's tail!' the guard exclaimed, watching the black-dyed lashes flutter about the blue eyes.

A handsome woman, even if she was past her prime, he considered. Her naked breasts and rouged cheeks proclaimed her calling, but the lines on her face were as yet only faintly etched and her dress was reasonably clean.

'I thought the daughter of Satan was already here,' she said pertly. 'Isn't Joan the witch girl held in one of your prisons?'

'She won't be there for much longer,' the soldier grinned. 'They're bringing her out today to sentence her.'

'Is that why the gates of the city are guarded?' she enquired.

'They've been guarded for months, ever since His Majesty King Henry arrived, but today nobody without a pass gets in or out of the city. They're bringing the witch out to the public cemetery, and there's always a chance of a rescue attempt.'

'Well, I'm not here to rescue her!' the girl flared. 'Give me half a chance and I'll light the faggots under her myself.'

'Why? Did she steal a lover of yours?'

'She ordered me from—well, that's none of your business! Just understand, she's no friend of mine.'

'And who might you be?'

'Bertha. And I don't have papers to prove it; and I don't

have a pass to get into the city, so what would you like to do about it?'

'I know what I'd like to do about *you*,' he said, eyeing her. 'But I'd have the skin flogged off my back if I left my post before sunset.'

'I could meet you when you come off duty,' she said, eagerly. 'I'd wait for you, if you'll let me in now.'

'It's risky without a pass,' he said, dubiously, but she rubbed her hand slowly down his jerkin, and he relented.

'Go in then and promise to return here at sunset.'

'Don't leave your post,' she whispered, and flashed past him into the narrow tangle of streets where an unusually large number of people were streaming in one direction. Most of them were tradesfolk, but there was a sprinkling of black-robed clergy and a fair proportion of soldiers. Normally, Bertha would have attached herself to one of the latter, but she was eager to reach her destination, and hurried in the wake of the crowds, pulling her shawl over her shoulders to forestall the threatened reproach of a monk who was staring at her indignantly.

Her first disappointed thought was that she had come too late to find a good place, for the walled graveyard was already crammed with spectators. Some of them were packed like sardines in the narrow spaces between the graves, while others clung to the tomb-stones or perched on the surrounding wall.

Then a couple of young men hoisted her up between them to the forked branch of a sturdy yew, and she could look over the heads of the crowd to the two platforms erected near the church.

One of the platforms was occupied by men in rich ecclesiastical robes and by several noblemen in bright velvets.

On the other platform, a priest stood opposite a figure seated on a stool. Bertha strained her eyes across the space, noting with satisfaction that the girl Joan wore a ragged doublet and hose, and that her face was half-

179

hidden by tangled elf-locks of black hair, so that she looked unkempt and ordinary.

I care nothing for what she once said of me, Bertha thought, viciously, and never bothered to ask herself why she should have troubled to come so far, to learn the fate of one for whose opinion she cared nothing.

The priest had begun to speak, and the crowd fell silent. Bertha, who had not been to church or listened to a sermon for years, yawned, and wondered why pious men so often talked through their noses. Her attention was jerked when the figure on the stool called out.

'By my faith,' Joan cried indignantly, 'my King is not as you say, but is the most noble of all Christians, who best loves the faith and the church!'

'Poor little devil!' the man next to Bertha muttered. 'She defends that poltroon Charles who hasn't raised a finger to save her.'

The priest was shouting her down, waving his finger in front of the prisoner's nose and sawing back and forth on his heels.

'There'll be trouble from the English if she escapes the flames,' said Bertha's companion, shifting closer to her so that the branch creaked ominously. 'She's caused them so much trouble that they'll not be content with anything less than death.'

The priests were asking the captive if she would submit to the Church, and the clear voice rose again.

'Let all my words and deeds be sent to our Holy Father, the Pope, to whom, after God, I refer myself. I have said and done everything through God, but if there is a fault in me, it is mine alone.'

There was another brief pause, and then a babble of voices as those on the platform began arguing and gesticulating. One of the priests had his hand on the girl's shoulder and was whispering earnestly in her ear. Some of the richly dressed English nobles were leaping to their feet. Then, as suddenly as it had arisen, the brief tumult died away. The most splendidly clad of the churchmen rose to his feet and his voice rolled out in sonorous phrases.

Ears were strained to catch the words of the formal excommunication and eyes strayed towards a cart waiting at the side. In this cart, the witch would ride after she had been cast out from the body of the Church and handed over to the secular arm for punishment.

The bishop had reached the main burden of his speech and his voice throbbed with the solemnity of his own eloquence.

'For these reasons we declare you excommunicate and heretical, and pronounce that you be abandoned to secular justice, as a limb of Satan, severed from the Church.'

The ragged figure had sprung to her feet and the bishop's deep voice was drowned by a shrill feminine one, that cried over and over, 'I submit! I submit! I will not listen to my voices again for they lied to me. They were false. False! False!'

From her high seat, Bertha watched with excitement as pandemonium broke out below her. Several women were screaming hysterically, urging on their menfolk to fling gravel and mud. The missiles struck some of the English guard below the rail of the platform, and there was a clash of steel as pikes were levelled. The dignified churchmen were scrambling between the two platforms, pulling themselves up between spaces in the rail. The priest who had whispered to Joan was trying to shield her with his cassock from flying lumps of earth. Another was reading something to her from a document, while somebody else was calling for a pen.

Confusion piled upon confusion and fights broke out in several parts of the crowd, punctuated by more screaming and the wailing of a small child separated from its mother in the crush.

Then Joan's voice was heard again. 'Men of the church, take me out of the hands of these English!'

Bishop Cauchon's tones overrode her. 'Take her back

to the place from which she came!'

He was trying to leave the platform, but one of the English lords had caught him by the arm and was hectoring him loudly. People were surging back and forth, their faces distorted like animals cheated of their prey. A few had begun to run back through the gates into the streets, shouting furiously and brandishing sticks.

'Best stay up here, lass,' advised the man, 'until the crowds have gone. There'll be a rare hullabaloo today, now that the witch has been recanted. The English are hot for another burning.'

'Another?'

'Aye. They burned some poor crazy girl last month. A prophetess or some such, called herself La Pierronne, and said the Maid was gentle and came from God. They hustled her to the stake in double-quick time.'

Bertha shifted her cramped leg, and tried to pick out the figure of the pucelle, but there were too many others crowding about the prisoner.

'I hoped to see a burning,' she said.

'Did you? Most men don't care for them, but women have stronger stomachs. For my part, I'm glad to see the English cheated. They've been cheating us for years—not that I'd venture that opinion too loudly. I have a nice little business in the town, and I've no wish to find all my stock smashed up. Are you a particular friend of the English?'

He looked at her sideways, as if fearing he had said too much.

'I'm everybody's particular friend,' Bertha said wryly. 'Except the witch girl, of course. I wanted to see her burn!'

'Well, she's as good as dead,' the man said, comfortably. 'Disgraced and sent to perpetual imprisonment. She'd be better off if they'd killed her. As it is, we can all laugh our heads off at those who followed her.'

Bertha had quite regained her cheerfulness and beamed as she accepted the citizen's helping hand down from the seat. He would have remained with her longer, but the press of people separated them and she was carried out of his reach.

She had promised to return to the guard at sunset and she usually kept her word; but meanwhile the sun was shining, the pucelle was disgraced, and Rouen was full of men. Bertha pulled the shawl from her bodice and fell into the slow, sauntering gait of her trade.

ROUEN, MAY, 1431

It was dark and cold in the little room, although a stray sunbeam occasionally fell through the barred window, lighting the pallet against the wall, the log of wood to which the prisoner's leg was chained, and the three bulky figures crouched over their dice game.

The Maid sat quietly, her hands folded over the neat brown dress they had given her. She was empty of all feeling except despair, for there was nothing within her mind except whirling darkness. There was no need for her to be hurt by the betrayal of others, because she had betrayed herself more terribly than anyone else could have done. For three days she had existed in limp apathy, and one question formed itself over and over in her brain. Why, when she had submitted to the judgement of Holy Mother Church, could she feel no joy?

Side by side with the question lay the answer. She felt no joy because in denying her voices she had denied the word of God.

A third question crept into her brain. Was there truly any God, or were the many words spoken about him lies and delusions? She moved further into the deep shadow, dropping her head on her hands. There is no God, ran the current of her thought, and if there is a God I will never see Him, for I have denied His Truth.

'Silly child!' said the voice, teasingly.

183

Her pulse beat more rapidly, and the voice came again, gentle and mocking.

'Silly child! Do you not yet believe that God loves you and will deal gently with you?'

She opened her hands, cupping the brilliant light between them, watching with hungry eyes the tiny golden figures.

'I betrayed you. Isn't God angry?'

'He sends us to tell you that He pities you, for having revoked and recanted what you knew to be the truth.'

'And what is my punishment to be?'

'No punishment, Joan,' said the voice. 'If you cut yourself off from God, then you are without Him. And to be without Him is to be in hell. But you go there of your own free will.'

'But I submitted to the Church.'

'Do you think Pierre Cauchon and the men he rules are the whole church? You used to have more sense.'

'Then why do you come to me? Why don't you leave me in the hell to which I sent myself?'

The laughter came again, and with it the scent of lilies, filling the room.

'Silly child! We are here to tell you that one chance remains. When that chance comes, and you are again asked if you will stand by your recantation, you must not deny us again. If you do, we will never return.'

'But they will burn me!' All the nightmares of childhood flashed through her mind.

'That is not important,' chimed the voices.

'They will say that I am mad!'

'That is of no importance, to you or to us,' the voices echoed.

'For there is joy to come,' repeated the one called Margaret.

'How can I tell? How will I know? How will it be?'

The tiny beings nodded at one another and smiled. The golden light spread beyond her fingers, bathing her face and body, and the air was full of bells and there was neither time nor space, only an eternal Now. And at the core of the radiance, a glimpse of Something ever changing, drawing into Itself the harmony of all created things.

'The pucelle is at her prayers again,' one of the guards remarked.

'She is forever at them,' another observed. 'I never saw a witch who spent so much time on her knees.'

'It's your turn,' the third said, impatiently.

'I'm sick of the game. And there's no profit in it.'

'If it's profit you're after,' said one, in a low tone, 'I know how we can make some money on the quiet, if you're willing to listen.'

'How?'

'The Earl of Warwick sent for me today. Can you guess what he wanted?'

'He asked you to join the Privy Council!' suggested one.

'He asked you if you had a cure for the pox, seeing you've had it so often yourself!' quipped the other.

'He asked me if I would like to earn a hundred crowns.'

'For what?'

'For playing a trick on the pucelle. She is to be allowed to take a bath tomorrow, and while she is in the bath, we are to take away her woman's dress and lay out tunic and hose for her.'

'What's the point of that?'

The soldier laughed, clapping the other on the shoulder.

'The Earl of Warwick and the Duke of Bedford want the Maid dead. But the churchmen say she has repented, and cannot be burned. Unless she breaks her promise to the church and puts on men's clothes again.'

'Be quiet, or she'll hear you,' said the one still holding the dice.

'She won't hear a thing. She's listening to another world!' his companion replied, and they laughed heartily at their own wit.

The town seethed with agitated, excited crowds, swayed by the wind of rumour from one extreme opinion to another. The pucelle was to be sewn up in a sack and thrown into the river. The pucelle was to be sent to Rome for the Holy Father wished to meet her. The pucelle was to be strangled in her cell, for she had threatened to reveal certain secrets. She had put on male garments again and a new trial had been ordered.

Giles, gulping his breakfast wine, grinned as he heard the ebb and flow of conversations about him. He had just spent two hours piling up logs and sticks and piles of green twigs, and knew very well where the pucelle was bound.

Rouen was packed so tightly that it was a wonder the walls didn't bulge outward. Giles knew that every Englishman in the town was expected to be on watch lest a possible rescue be attempted. There had been trouble already between groups of English and French, and Bishop Cauchon had called out his personal guard for his own protection. Priests and lawyers, noble lords and prelates had been coming and going all morning, in and out of the prison. Two of the priests had come away in tears muttering their prayers as their sandalled feet brushed the cobbles.

Giles finished his drink and shouldered his way out of the tavern, laying about him with his cudgel as he went, to clear a pathway through the mob. There were so many Englishmen in the crowd that if he had closed his eyes he might almost have thought himself at home.

He decided that when his spell of duty was up he might go home again. His mother was dead and weeds grew up around the door of the old hut, but it would be pleasant to see his brothers again. So thinking, he elbowed his way back into the square.

The stake was already in position and one of Giles's colleagues was hammering a painted board into the ground.

'Please, soldier!' A hand tugged at his jerkin. 'Can you read the words on that board?'

Giles shook his head curtly, but a monk, moving to the platform erected nearby, stopped and spelled them out.

> ' "Joan who called herself pucelle, liar,
> pernicious deceiver of the people,
> superstitious, blasphemer, presumptuous,
> disbeliever in the faith, boastful, idolatrous,
> cruel, dissolute, invoker of devils, apostate,
> schismatic, and heretic." '

It sounded, considered Giles, even more damning in French, than in honest English. He disliked foreign tongues and, despite having picked up a fairly wide knowledge of French, was still convinced that his native speech was the purest and the most practical.

There was a distant muttering that swelled to a roar and the monk, mumbling that he must get to his place for they were bringing out the devil-woman, hurried away.

The platforms were filling up, with Bishop Cauchon, disdainfully aristocratic, inclining his head curtly towards the other judges as they took their seats. The Earl of Warwick, in chain-mail as if he were preparing for battle, had cast a swift, considering look at the English clustered about the stake, and then leaned back in his chair with a bored expression on his face.

There came the rattling of wheels and then the executioner's cart, surrounded by pikemen, lumbered slowly into the market-place.

'It's said that the girl was tricked into putting male dress on again,' said a woman, craning her neck as the prisoner was led down to the space before the judges.

There was a hint of sympathy in her voice that caused Giles to glance at her sharply. For the first time, he realized that the crowds in the square were unusually silent. There was no sound, save the high-pitched voice of the priest giving an exhortation, and an occasional isolated comment from a member of the spectators.

Giles had caught one or two distant glimpses of the devil-girl, as she was being taken to and from her cell for questioning; but for the first time he felt a lively curiosity about her. He had attended several executions, but had never been conscious before of this uneasiness in the waiting crowd.

The priest was casting out the devil-woman now, abandoning her to the secular authorities. The prisoner, thought Giles, was certainly vociferous.

She had sunk to her knees and her voice was rising and falling in a kind of chant. He caught the name of Saint Michael and somebody in the crowd groaned, like a pitying echo.

The Bishop was rising, drawing his cape about him and beginning to speak the final sentence, but the resonant tones faltered. For an instant, Cauchon's proud face bore an odd, listening expression. Then he made a hasty gesture with his arm and sat down abruptly, shielding his eyes with his hand.

The guards were seizing her and propelling her towards the stake. Two black-habited priests were trying to accompany her. The people in the square had begun to rock back and forth, and several women had already fainted and been dragged to the side.

The girl was bound to the stake now, with a breeze fluttering the edge of her sackcloth garment. Her voice rose again.

'I fear that Rouen will suffer for my death!'

The executioner was having difficulty in kindling the faggots. One of the priests was sobbing with his hands to his face; the other was trying to struggle through the guards with a crucifix. Giles looked up briefly to the white faced girl and at that moment her eyes turned towards him.

I have lived through this moment before, he thought.

Once, I saw blue eyes that looked through me to a world I could not see. I cannot remember the time or the place, but I remember the eyes, with the iris so intensely blue that it appeared black. He glanced down at his hands, curved as if they held a bowl of soup, and knowledge flickered, and died.

He bent down and pulled two twigs from the fast-smouldering pyre, and bound them into a cross with a loose thread from his tunic, and thrust the cross up to the girl, and turned away feeling as if he had just repaid a debt.

DOMREMY, JUNE, 1431

'Her heart would not burn,' Jacques d'Arc said.

He had been repeating the phrase over and over for days, until the words had lost all meaning. He sat indoors, with the shutters pulled close and the neighbours tiptoed in and out, whispering, as if he were an invalid.

'Her heart would not burn,' he said again, and tears ran down his face.

'And it would not drown,' said Zabillet. 'They put it in a box made of lead and threw it into the Seine, and the box floated.'

'But Joan is dead and will not return,' Jacques said heavily. 'She is dead and I, too, will soon be dead. Dead, buried, and forgotten! And she might have been safely wed by now if you had not persuaded me to allow her to stay at Vaucouleurs, so that she might bother Sir Robert de Baudicourt to let her go to Chinon.'

Zabillet opened her mouth to protest, but her husband had sunk back into his lethargy of grief. Instead, she went out to the garden at the side of the house and began to pull bind-weed from the bed of marjoram. She had neglected the weeding in recent months, and neglected her own appearance, too, so that she with greying hair and stained apron and the garden with straggling, unwatered plants had the same unkempt, unloved aspect.

'Is your husband better today?'

It was Hauviette with her baby in her arms, pausing by the low wall to speak in hushed, respectful tones.

'He will never be better,' Zabillet said, 'but sits and broods, while his plough rusts in the meadow and the sheep wander unchecked through the grain.'

'He loved Joan very much,' Hauviette said, tiredly.

'And didn't I love her, too? Didn't I carry her for nine months, and suckle her, and teach her to walk, and listen to her first words? Only to have her ride away to battle and never come home again.'

'She didn't say good-bye to me,' Hauviette mourned. 'I was one of her dearest friends and she left without a word. To be burnt alive as a heretic!'

'By Bishop Cauchon of Beauvais!' Zabillet intoned, viciously pulling the head off an unoffending daisy.

Hauviette had turned to watch a figure plodding towards them.

'I wonder what Jean Morel wants,' she wondered aloud. 'He must have walked from Greux.'

'He offered to come over to talk to Jacques. To try to rouse him a little from his sorrow.'

Zabillet stood up, brushing the soil from her dress. The baby started to wail lustily and Hauviette looked down with self-conscious pride.

'Feeding-time again! This child is never satisfied, I swear! I'd best be off home.'

She shifted the weight of the infant from one side to the other, bobbed politely as she passed Morel, and hurried along the road.

'It's good of you to keep your promise, Jean,' Zabillet greeted him.

'No trouble! At times like these, we must help one another.'

She was glad that there was no trace in his expression of the furtive excitement she had noticed in the faces of some of those who had come to condole.

'I brought something with me, so I'm glad to find you alone,' Morel was saying.

'Something for me?'

'I hope I'm doing right in bringing it, but my wife thought you'd like to have it; but it might upset Jacques too much.'

'Is this it?'

Zabillet took the bundle from the stammering Morel, and pulled off the coverings.

'It's Joan's old dress. She gave it to me at Rheims when we travelled there for the Coronation. I thought—that is, my wife thought, that you'd like something of hers.'

'It was very kind,' Zabillet managed to say, forcing steadiness into her voice.

Morel patted her awkwardly on the shoulder.

'We thought it would be nice for you to have something to remember her by,' he said, going towards the house.

But I don't need it, Zabillet thought. Faded red cloth won't bring back her memory to me. Joan has gone and will never return. They will all forget her, despite their mourning and their weeping, and their sympathetic words.

Then her mouth tightened and she lifted up her head.

'I will appeal against the verdict,' she said aloud. 'I will not allow my daughter to be forgotten. I will not allow her memory to be thrust, dishonoured, out of sight. If necessary, I'll go to the Holy Father himself to beg for justice.'

She pushed the dress back into its wrappings, and laid the parcel carefully on top of the wall. Then she continued with the weeding, while to her nostrils floated the scent of lilies where lilies had never grown.

THE END

AUTHOR'S NOTE

All the main incidents in the foregoing novel are true, and all the characters really existed, although I have taken the liberty of giving names to Giles, Simon, and Bertha, for their original names have not been recorded. To avoid confusion, I have also called the main characters by those terms by which they are most familiar to English readers, so the girl whose name was spelt variously as Jeanne, Jehan, Joanna, and Jehanne, is known here simply as Joan.

For those who like to know how the story ended—Jacques d'Arc died broken-hearted a few years after the execution, but Zabillet d'Arc retired to Orleans and there petitioned the Pope for an enquiry into her daughter's trial. One of Joan's brothers became Governor of Vaucouleurs, and the other founded a large family. Dunois and d'Alençon died full of years and honours. Gilles de Raiz was hanged for the ritual murder of over a hundred children. And King Henry VI of England was eventually deposed and murdered by Edward IV.

The others moved into the shadows of history, but the figure of Joan, enigmatic and compelling, remains.